BFS Horizons
#16

FICTION EDITOR
Pete Sutton

ASSISTANT EDITOR
Nadya Mercik

POETRY EDITOR
Ian Hunter

LAYOUT
Zena Wilde

the british fantasy society

About the Cover Artist

Jenni Coutts is a speculative fiction writer, illustrator, and junior doctor based in Glasgow, Scotland. She was shortlisted for the Scottish Book Trust's New Writer's Awards 2019, and has been a member of Glasgow SF Writer's Circle since 2014. Some of her more notable achievements include becoming an elderly cat rescuer, avid gardener, and night shift queen.
For more information, visit jennicoutts.com

First published in the UK in 2023 by

The British Fantasy Society

www.britishfantasysociety.co.uk

BFS Horizons © 2023 The British Fantasy Society

Contents

Editorial

Welcome to issue 16 of BFS Horizons, the first issue where we are paying contributors for their stories, poems, and artwork, this is another major milestone in the history of the Society, and I look forward to reading the stories, especially the winner and runner ups of the BFS Short Story Prize 2022, and looking over the artwork with envy.

Amongst the poems in this issue is one from the late Clint Wastling, a member of the society and a regular at the Fantasycon Poetry Open mic, and other online events. Check out issue 14 for his three poems "Specimen", "Post Mortem" and "Stone Circle". Those who knew Clint can easily hear his distinct tones delivering them. He had a great voice, and as a poet knew which words to choose and where to put them, as well as having a pretty cool first name. He will be missed.

As ever, thanks to Pete Sutton for all his help in assembling Horizons, and Shona and the rest of the Committee, particularly for doing a brilliant job in putting on last year's Fantasycon, which I thought was a very hands-on affair, from a writer's point of view although I still don't have my online presence sorted out — yet. I hope to see you in Birmingham this year where I shall be putting my trusty John Aitken Fantasycon Pub Map to good use. Look out for me, I'll be the guy with the tattered map with scribbled notes all over it, and hopefully John won't get locked in the Indian restaurant across from the Jury's Inn, this time.

Ian Hunter, *South Lanarkshire, March 2023*

Miniatures
by Lisa Farrell

I had become known for my miniatures, my lovers' eyes in particular. Once society decided I was the best there was for such portraits, I became inundated with clients from all over town. Ladies and gentlemen both appeared at my door, desirous to have their gazes captured and rendered portable. I painted eyes of all shapes and colours; loving eyes, yearning eyes and sultry eyes, even suspicious eyes for husbands to hang from chains at their wives' necks.

My trick was very simple. It was to paint them as true to life as my skill allowed, and though called "miniatures", I even copied the dimensions of those features as accurately as I could. So when a gentleman slipped his lover's eye from an envelope or pocket for a moment, however fleeting, his mind might perceive a real eye laying there on his palm. He would not be fooled long of course, but though his senses overcame that first perception the mystique remained.

Stories began to circulate that a man had really "seen" his wife's adultery in his sleep, as she had foolishly discarded his painted eye broach with her clothes on the bedroom floor, and that a wronged woman had cursed her unfaithful lover, by sending him the image of her frowning blue eye. These tales only spread my reputation further, but whether there was any truth in them I could not say. I may have painted such an accusing blue eye, I had painted so many. I could not be expected to remember them all.

Yet their images, which I had taken such pains to produce, did linger somewhere in my mind. They would appear in my dreams, eyes watching me from every angle. I began to see them on waking too, in a reflection of light in the bowl where I washed, or on the blade of my razor when I shaved.

I would blow out my candle at night only to glimpse eyes in the darkness, begging me to view them in a way no one else could, to capture and collect them like butterflies. It was exhausting.

Still, I let the sitters come. I was making my fortune after all, and it is hard to refuse vast sums of money. I increased my prices, and only gained richer clients. Some began to come secretly, their faces masked, only their eyes visible. Others had retinues of servants in attendance, though I insisted these remained outside. I was growing superstitious in my habits, and the process of capturing those eyes felt too intimate a process to be observed. There would be only two gazes in the room; the sitter's gaze and mine, my practised, artist's gaze that examined theirs and reproduced it.

As my wealth grew, I became more suspicious. I hired guards and servants to manage the callers who climbed up the stairs to my rooms. I began to see my gift as something more than mere skill; I began to see a power behind it, something spiritual. I increased my prices further, and still they came. The magic of my brush never failed me. I felt I had been given a great gift, and I fancied lovers around the world exchanged their miniatures that I had painted. I imagined a world without adultery, wherein every man and woman could watch their lovers from afar and keep them chaste.

Yet I knew this to be fantasy. In my darkest hours, I despaired that I left no legacy. I would hardly be remembered as a great artist, for mere unsigned miniatures. Moreover, the work was taking its toll and I still felt watched by staring eyes wherever I went, whatever I did. At the end of one long day's work, I threw down my brush and vowed to paint no more of those miniatures that so taxed my powers. I would paint something else; a full portrait perhaps, or the scene from my window. Yes, that was it; I would paint something without any eyes in it at all. I would paint a masterpiece, and I would be remembered for it.

I woke that night with a distinct feeling that I was observed. I felt the heat of a gaze upon me; I was watched not passively, but intensely scrutinised. I opened my eyes to see the glint of another's at the end of my bed, eerily bright like a cat's, and a figure appeared like shadows gathering.

"I have come for a portrait," came the whisper. "I want you to paint me a miniature."

The figure turned and went through into my workshop where the lamps were burning bright, though I was sure I had extinguished them before I slept.

I might have been afraid at the intrusion, or angry at the visitor's presumption, but somehow all I could think of was how I might capture the metallic glint of their eye, and how it might look immortalised upon ivory. Only hours before, I had resolved to give up such work. Now, it was what I lived for once again.

The figure sat ready in a chair, and I saw that they carried the darkness with them in the form of a black cloak and hood. It enveloped their body and shadowed their face, so all I saw was that one golden eye, and that was fixed upon me.

I set to work at once, trying to get the perfect blend of lead-tin yellow, burnt umber and vermilion to imitate the flashing gold of the iris. The form of the eye was easy, such a perfectly symmetrical almond shape, my brush happily followed that smooth curve. The pupil, however, was the biggest challenge. That sphere of blackness seemed to contain more detail the longer I gazed into its depths. There were cities of marble, glittering under a bright sun, pleasure barges floating along curvaceous rivers, and golden statues reaching fingers towards a cloudless sky. I saw whole worlds contained within that eye, and though I must work with the tip of a pin, I was determined to illustrate all I could.

I painted until I could paint no more, and though I felt such ecstasy when I gazed upon the finished piece, such flushing gratitude when I showed my sitter and received the whispered praise, a strange longing remained. I knew I would never paint such an eye again.

"May I paint your other one?" I ventured.

"I only require this portrait," the whisper came, and a feminine hand, white as bone, emerged from the darkness of those robes. Long fingers opened to reveal gold coins, enough to pay for the work a hundred times over.

"Instead of payment," I said. "Let me paint your other eye, and keep the image for myself."

The laugh that came was like the wheezing of a dying man.

"As you wish."

I readied my materials and clutched my brush eagerly. This miniature would be my greatest work, which I would set in gold and diamonds.

The fingers closed again over the gold, and the figure turned so that I could see the second eye. Silver flashed, bright but cold as sunlight on snow. As I painted the iris my very blood seemed to cool, the lamps dimmed, and my gaze caught on something hidden in the darkness of the pupil.

I saw bare black branches clutching at a white sky, thick smoke bursting from cracks in barren earth, and stone roads where only the dead walked, leading away into tunnels underground. I heard the click, click, click of skeletal feet on stone and I tore my eyes away, squeezed them closed.

The wheezing laugh came again.

"You must finish soon," she whispered. "It is almost dawn."

I did not look again at the eye, but at my work, trying to take what was in my memory and paint it, hoping that I might then forget what I had seen. By the time I looked up again the lamps had burnt out, the room was flooded with the still, cold light of dawn, and the figure was gone.

I looked down at the silvery eye I had painted; its gaze seemed to tear through me, exposing all my pride to myself. It was an unflinching, haunting gaze and I wanted to escape it, to dash it to the floor and smash it to a thousand pieces. Yet, something stayed my hand. This miniature was still the second-finest work I had ever produced. I turned my back on it and took to my bed.

I couldn't sleep, thinking of that eye staring, unblinking from my workbench. I knew that if I closed my eyes I would dream of that dead world I glimpsed in the darkness behind it, of white bones and black emptiness, of gaping sockets and the bleak vistas of the underworld. I felt the world outside, where the morning sun shone, as a hollow image, a thin veneer on reality. Death was the only, inevitable, permanence.

I heard one of my servants enter the workshop, their steps quick upon the floorboards. A pause, as they noticed the miniature left on the workbench. I imagined them looking down into the depths of the pupil I painted, and learning the truth as I had.

I thought that perhaps if another soul stared into that dead eye, they would live in its thrall instead of me.

"You can have it!" I called out. "Take it away!"

There was no answer. I rose and returned to my workshop, where the servant stood at the workbench. The young man looked up at me with taut, frightened eyes that had glimpsed darkness.

"You can have it," I said again, but he shook his head.

As I looked on him, his youthful flush drained from his cheeks, and I saw the fate that awaited him like a shadow behind his eyes. I saw his jawbone crumble, his face sink in on itself as the corruption crept upwards and ate away his nose, leaving a rotten hole. I could not bear to look further and turned away to the window.

The servant had raised the shutters, and already the street outside was filling with a flow of people. Traders and shoppers, gentlemen and ladies, masters and servants. All ignorant of the shadow they lived under, the emptiness that awaited them. A girl selling flowers opposite looked up at me, and though our glances met only fleetingly I saw her flesh fall away and sores erupt across her skin, her raw throat and bloodied gums. I pulled the shutters closed, blocking out the bustle of the street.

"I want no more clients," I said, without turning around. "I will paint no more miniatures. Send them all away."

The servant ran from the room, and the latch clattered down as the door slammed shut. I locked it at once, knowing solitude was my only refuge. My gift was corrupted; it seemed I could not look into another eye without seeing the horrendous death that awaited. There were so many ways to die, and I did not want to bear witness to them all.

Clients still came knocking for a while, but I kept the door locked, and eventually, they stopped. I placed a cloth over the silver eye and set up my old easel to work. I have never painted another miniature since, only the scenes that haunt my waking dreams. Only leafless trees, empty skies, and hollow skulls. Such is my gift.

Lisa Farrell studied English at York and Creative Writing at the UEA, then spent seven years working in bookshops before withdrawing from civilized society to start a family. She now juggles her motherly duties with the compulsion to write fantastical, speculative, and weird fiction. She also writes freelance for *Fantasy Flight Games*. Follow @lisamrc8 or visit lisafarrell.blogspot.co.uk

Godzilla At The Pow Wow

by Juan Manuel Perez

drumbeat, drumbeat, drum
a deep rhythmic rumbling sound
music from the heart

he shows up sometimes
after messing up a place
to cool himself off

drumbeat, drumbeat, drum
back since the Astro-Monster
dancing for the win

dancing for his life
dancing for it is sacred
dancing for prayer

drumbeat, drumbeat, drum
he must be part NDN
puts him in a trance

pow wows aren't the same
without a kaiju stomp dance
peyote puff clouds

drumbeat, drumbeat, drum
reminds him of something gone
he never says what

Juan Manuel Perez is a Mexican-American of Indigenous descent and the author of multiple books of poetry. Juan currently resides in Corpus Christi, Texas. To learn more about him, visit his official website at: https://www.juanmperez.com/

The Ghost Of You

by Dave Jeffery

The spoon is back. It's there – resting on the mug, an equator of silver crossing the dark, liquid void, straddling the brim, handle on one side, scoop on the other, the tea brewing beneath as dark as this feeling in my heart.

This is how it is, now. Little mysteries – hints that things are not quite how they were; subtle shadows of foreboding but with sharp edges, needling my consciousness, making sure that I can never forget what has been lost to me.

Marianne.

She is gone but not prepared to be forgotten, it seems. Not by a mystic mile. She was a strong and persistent soul even in life. Now Death has taken a hand, and we are both its courtesan.

The home we built together is nothing special, but it is ours – was ours – and into it we poured our hopes and dreams; the little money we had burgeoned by poignant aspiration. The days we spent walking in the park, hand in hand; the heady sound of her laughter on the air; the quiet moments as we both became lost in a good book and supped strong tea or coffee, beer and wine. Days courting the sun, nights sharing the wanton, our bodies warming each other, fulfilling each other, embraced or entwined, an eternal sense of somatic and emotive harmony.

"Live for the moment," Marianne would often say, but it is these very words that haunt me now.

Well, perhaps not *just* the words, not recently.

There is something else, something with *substance,* something

14

capable of placing a spoon on a mug, the way she always used to do when brewing tea. She knows it infuriates me, the metal is always hot when you go back after the tea bag has brewed for its customary three minutes, no more – no less. The number of times I've burnt my fingers and cursed the air is countless.

Like the minutes that have passed since we were ripped apart from one another.

Truth is always important, these days, more than ever.

When I first met Marianne, it wasn't love at first sight, we both admitted that to each other later – when we were certain that we were always going to be together. We believed such conviction; love made us impervious to anything life could throw at us.

Look how that turned out.

But our connection went deeper than mere aesthetics. Our first meeting involved a calamity, but from disaster something magnificent emerged, something ever long.

I was waiting tables in a tearoom, my way of supplementing my maintenance grant as I studied English Literature and Creative Writing at University of Birmingham. Marianne was reading, her small frame made even more delicate by the size of the armchair. My eyes flitted from her plain features to the abstract cover of her book, a well-worn copy of *Wuthering Heights*. She didn't look up.

I gave a cough, against my instinct as an avid reader, and I feared I had now become a destroyer of worlds. For a brief moment, I saw her deep brown eyes go through changes, struggling to adjust as she was wrenched from her literary realm, then garnering recognition to their surroundings as she reluctantly returned to reality, followed by the brief-but-intense second of irritation she gave to me before seeing the tray I carried. Her smile came swift, warm and welcoming.

I gave her my customer-service smile. "Sorry to disturb you. Did you order the pesto/cheese panini and pot of English breakfast?"

I knew she had; the table number corresponded with my server slip.

But there was something about her that made me feel unsure of myself, and I used the statement to give me chance to steady the nerves.

Her face retained its amity. "Yes, I did. Thank you." After a pause, she added, "Although you're going to have trouble finding somewhere to park it."

She pointed out the issue with a nod of her head, the table hadn't been cleared after use by a previous customer. In my head, I cursed Mickey another under grad who had been waiting this section of tables prior to handing it over to me and going off-shift.

"Okay. Sorry about that. I'll get that cleared for you."

I made to go back to the counter, but Marianne had placed her book on the seat next to her and was already moving things around, placing them on the tray that had been left behind, plates and cups clattering as she did so.

She lifted the laden tray free of the table, allowing me to set mine down.

I gave her a nod. "Very efficient. You should work here."

She held her tray out to me and gave me a wink. "So should you."

A soft, sophisticated reprimand which I took in the spirit of its delivery by pulling an 'ouch' face. This earned me a brief smile and I think that was the moment I saw the true person behind the consumer façade for the first time. My gut tingled with excitement when her eyes sparkled under the overheads.

But as I took the tray, the instant destined to bring us together for the next ten years happened. A precariously placed teacup, teetered and fell onto its side, spilling its cold, dark contents, a brown waterfall that slopped over the edges of the tray and onto Marianne's copy of *Wuthering Heights*.

With a squeal, she tried to rescue the book, but the cover was soaked, the pages stained and already curling as she snatched it from the chair.

Panicked, I turned and went for the serving counter, calling behind me. "Oh, I'm so sorry."

I expected fire, a retort that would have me branded. Instead, when I returned to the table with a handful of paper towels, she was gone.

I can hear Marianne on the breeze. She is singing "Amazing Grace", her favourite hymn. It is the lullaby taught to her by her mother. Marianne often sings it when she is rueful and feeling nostalgic, and it carries with it an everlasting layer of melancholy. She was always singing – and laughing, of course – and both were music to me, a happy symphony composed from her simple joy of life. How I loved to hear her, how it felt as her soft falsetto cupped and held my heart, how I wept when I thought I would never hear that voice again.

But now it is back, I am torn where I was once healed, and the song is always the same, that infernally unhappy refrain, drifting from downstairs when I am in the lounge, or rising through the floorboards when I am in the bedroom. That song, a signature for her sadness, and I long to look upon her yet fear it at the same time.

Is this madness, I ask of myself often, *are there dark voices to follow those iridescent chords?*

I shiver, cold at the thought of where all of this is going. The seeds of doubt grow into a forest of uncertainty, of who I am, who I was, who I'll be without her in my life. The future is now a smudged horizon, forever impossible to define.

Loneliness hurts like a sliver of glass embedded in my palm.

Marianne had been on my mind since the day she'd walked out of the tearoom, and I found the intensity of these thoughts so odd that I feared the guilt of my act had made me a little obsessive. All I could recall was those brown eyes, wide open in horror as her beloved book was warped by my carelessness.

Almost immediately I'd sought out another copy of *Wuthering Heights* to give to her should I ever see her again. The thought that I may not ever get the opportunity left me empty and, upon reflection, there was a very real chance that I was in love with her even in that short space of time. I'd never seen her in the tea shop before, and part of me thought that after her book was ruined, the chances of her coming back were slim.

But I continued with my search regardless, researching the best edition to purchase without crippling my meagre maintenance grant. Despite the chances of it ever actually happening, the need to see her and put this thing right grew until it became so incredibly important, I began dreaming about it, about her, and the response I would receive should it ever truly happen.

Most of what I fancied was negative, of course. A rebuff, a concerned look in those beautiful eyes indicating that she saw my madness as though I wore it as a mask. Still, perspective came with contemplation, and rational thinking. It wasn't wrong to want to set the balance of things. This was a woman with no name and a deep appreciation of gothic romance, of love and obsession and tragedy. The irony alone should woo her forgiveness.

Still, after many nights trawling the internet, I found a copy of Bronte's classic in hard back from *The Folio Society*, a reasonably priced affair, beautifully illustrated by artist *Rovina Cai*. When it arrived, I was almost afraid to open it, but the scent of wood pulp rising from the pages lured me in. Not wanting to mark the pages, I wrote a note on a post it and slipped it inside:

To the girl with no name
From the man with no sense of balance!
 x

I took the tome and wrapped it in brown paper, stowing it in my work locker in the hope that I would see her again. But it was several weeks before she came into the tearoom, at a time when I'd almost given up hope. When she sat down at her table, I went to my locker, where I retrieved the book and made an attempt to regain composure.

If she bore any malice from our previous meeting, she did not show it when she looked up at me as I stood by her table. Her smile came readily, and my heart was shimmying in my chest, making me feel like a kid going in for his first prom kiss.

I presented the package. "I have something for you."

"I don't recall ordering a present."

"Call it a replacement."

I placed the parcel on the table. She looked at it but made no move to touch it.

It was at that point I felt the need to explain. "It's just a book."

"I figured that much. But why?"

"I ruined the other one."

She shrugged. "This is true. But it was an accident. I bought another."

My heart sank, perhaps I had misjudged its importance in her life.

"Well, that's just my way of saying sorry."

"Then I accept your apology."

There was relief at this, and I nodded my own thanks.

Those eyes were on me again. "Can I ask you something?"

I was so relieved. My response was rapid. "Of course."

"Can I get a pot of tea at some point in the next hour?"

Her smile was infectious, and I took her order chuckling.

I was changing coffee filters behind the counter as she got up and walked out of the tearoom. On her way past, she gave me a tentative wave, the unopened packet under her arm. I confess that I was disappointed that she'd not sought to open it, but part of me was content that I'd done what I could to set things straight.

Later that evening, my shift done and my collar turned up in preparation for the brisk winds of winter, I left the shop. Marianne was standing outside, big coat, scarf looking like a multi-coloured boa constrictor about her neck. Before I'd realised any meaning, she was hugging me tight. We parted after a few seconds.

The kiss lasted longer.

There is a warm breeze on my neck and its heat is stark, dragging me into the moment. The bedroom is, as always, chilly and unforgiving in this seemingly endless winter to which I have now subscribed. It makes the breeze more obvious, even more potent, and I know its origins as sure as I know I should react with more gusto than I actually do.

Marianne has made her existence felt again and I cannot deny that fear does play a part as I hug myself and ponder on what all of this means. It is not as though I reject her presence, but there are questions to be asked, answers that are never forthcoming. How can this be happening, and what do I do about it?

There is another concern, and it involves the power of grief and loss over the mind, and the influence of madness. I shut the door on this as soon as these tenets turn up to the party.

Things are already bad enough. But I must admit, sometimes escaping from the reality of now has its appeal.

True love, the kind that lasts, is not fettered by the corporeal. It digs under the shallowness of aesthetics, seeking out and connecting with a kind heart and good soul beneath, the elements that refine and gives hint as to a person's true worth. And, just as time allowed us to mine each other's pasts – unlocking secrets and laying ourselves wide open to each other – so it was that Marianne and I became partners in time, inseparable, slaves to literature and the arts, travelling whenever and wherever we could in order to pander to such pursuits. Marriage, of course, was a natural progression, though in the early days neither of us were in any desperate rush to stand beneath such a banner. We were too busy revelling in other things, content and at peace.

On balance, maybe the universe had decided our fate back then, having too much in too short a space of time perhaps creating the kind of cosmic instability that derailed the order of things, meaning that the only way to regain equilibrium was to take a piss on our fledgling, passionate parade.

From a great, great height.

Cancer is more than a disease. It is nature's malice made real.

The diagnosis came after several weeks of ignoring the little things. Colon cancer is often called the silent killer, taking years to develop, but the clues were there if those concerned chose to look at them and the implications. The biggest failure wasn't that of malfunctioning organs but the will to communicate such things to the person that mattered the most. Once the news was out, we were both in a denial of sorts, retreating into a shell of contemplation and what-ifs .

The medics laid things out before us, the prognosis – with treatment, without treatment – things didn't really matter because the outcome was always going to be the same. There were discussions around 'quality of life', chemotherapy, and palliative care .

For seven months the spectre of cancer was always hovering on the periphery of our lives, while the discussions, no matter how much we tried, became dominated by this reality.

Yes, there were tensions and arguments and tears – of pain, of joy, of lost moments – but there was always love. We made promises to each other, of how life was to be when the inevitable happened. Neither of us meant to lie to the other. It was just that, when the time finally came, neither of us seemed to comprehend what pain truly was until its grip turned the screw.

The back wall of our living room is a beechwood shelving unit, floor to ceiling – books grace the entire space. They are arranged alphabetically, and I often said to Marianne that we lived in a bookshop.

She would put on a mock-accent. "I'll thank you to say 'library', you capitalist heathen." And we would laugh.

But she wasn't wrong, she barely ever was and not just in a 'lack of insight' kind of way. The room has an oppressive, erudite air about it, a place of reflection and learning and getting lost in the words of others.

Oh, what magic it is to weave wonders with words.

Since the time of her loss, this library has felt her presence on more than one occasion. Just like the other rooms, when I enter, I just perceive the very air has changed, the ghost of her perfume on the air, the sensation that she is standing nearby, watching me, wanting to reach out and take my hand.

God, how I miss the moments when I could hold her tight, feel her breath on my neck, the warmth of her hair on my cheek.

God. How. I. Miss. Her.

If there is a hell, then it is here, and I am living it.

The final days were a collage of senses, images of drip-feeds and a body so thin, the bones were defined like a trainee-orthopaedic surgeon's wet dream. Eyes, once so alive with the love of life, were dulled by its inexorable finality. Smells too, the hospital stink of disinfectant and alcohol wipes, the subtle undercurrent of necrosis and faeces.

And death, always and forever, death.

Hand in hand, fingers like fallen twigs wrapped in tissue paper, in danger of being crushed if held too tightly, body becoming the bed, the bed becoming an altar upon which life is sacrificed to the endless beyond.

Afterwards, the tears were there for such a long time, I cannot remember a time when my eyes have seen anything else.

Shame is my badge of office during this tenure. The days following the passing of life unto death, the funeral, the sequencing is just a haze of disconnected images, of tears and numbness, anger and a depth of despair never thought possible, hollowing out the soul the way a monger guts a fish.

Yet, although time is a gallery of raw, painful images, it is love that created the guiding light, heralding serenity with its deft touch, bleeding through, seeping into each canvas, until there is only one pigment, beautiful and mesmerising in its visceral might.

Can two people be so in love they are one and the same? I never thought such a thing possible but at times it felt right that we were not disparate entities, but united so that we were the cosmos, where existence is redefined, and losing one another would be like losing a limb, or giving in to the darker parts of your mind.

It was certainly the case that the loss of my Marianne was indeed like having my very soul ripped away, the days blunted, meaningless things, crammed only with the realities of what was no longer there.

Jesus, the emptiness, a mind sucked dry of hope, a body drained of energy; a husk that felt as though a mere breeze would have it crumbling to ash.

Perhaps it is the memory of such times that kept me from thinking I am courting madness when I sense her presence. She is here, of that I am convinced, in the house, in our garden, the greenhouse where she loved to spend so much time, nurturing her plants, sleeves rolled up and fronds of mousy hair escaping from her baseball cap.

When I step into each room, there is always the feeling that I have just missed her, the tantalising sense that she is just out of reach but close enough to make her mark on this empty, limbo world in which I now find myself.

And, in the space between, the ache in my heart mixed with the potent excitement of hope, and I am left overwhelmed by an emotion difficult to define, a hybrid the like of which I'm not sure I want to endure.

Damn it, I can do without guilt pulling up on the drive.

There is a sound on the night air, and I know it is Marianne softly weeping. Sadness punches my gut, the weight of not being able to offer comfort almost has my body riveted to the spot. The sound of sadness builds, sobs shiver the air, allowing me to seek her out, but there is always a good chance that this will be fruitless; by the time I locate the direction and isolate the source, she is never there.

So it is now, I move from the kitchen to the conservatory, a place of wicker furniture and plants with broad leaves, and see the copy of *Wuthering Heights* I bought for her has moved from the bookshelf and is now sitting on the rattan-framed coffee table. It is turned to the first page and I can see my handwriting.

After our kiss outside the tearoom, Marianne had me inscribe the same message directly into the book. As I look down, I can see there are two spots of water on the pages, and I am dumbfounded. Teardrops sink into the page as I realise their implication. I have literally just missed her, but this time she has left behind something tangible.

Movement to my left has me reeling. Beyond the panes of glass, shimmering under the light of a quarter moon, there is a figure outside in the garden. I hesitate, she is showing herself to me for the first time in what seems like a lifetime. I will finally get to look upon her, but I am at once fearful of what I will see.

This infernal disease has left such a stain on our lives, I wonder if it will have faded now it has taken all it can.

I go to the conservatory door, pass through, and there she is standing on the lawn, eyes streaming as she hugs herself.

Then, she speaks.

Her words lilt as though they have become the lyrics of a song, coming to me from far, far away. "I'm to blame. For all of it."

I step towards her, agonised when I see the desolation etched into her blanched face. "No. No. Please don't say that."

She is looking at me, but it is as though her focal point is on something beyond. "I know you're here. I've sensed you for such a long time. Damn it, I've taken comfort from it, but you're here because I can't let go. But I must. I *must* let you pass."

"No."

It is a response to her desperate words but also an understanding of the state of things. I am at once besieged by images and recollections – her face when I come clean and tell her I have been bleeding from my rectum for quite some time, ignoring the hard, hollow pain in my stomach, the loss of appetite making it so obvious there's a problem that she has confronted me about what the hell is going on. The words of the medics who tell me I have stage three colon cancer, now inoperable because my cowardice has made sure it's far too late. The infinite nausea of chemo, the pain, the agony as my insides are eaten away, turning my organs to black, stinking tissue that oozes from every pore until it is now the cologne I wear, until, thanks to the morphine, I die in an agonised slumber.

She has been there throughout, taken in the anger and the horror of watching me die. Now, it seems, we have both shared the delusion of life carrying on.

I say the words, but I realise she cannot hear them. "I'm scared."

"You are a good, beautiful man. Don't be afraid." It is a statement, not a response, a memory of who she knew me to be. But I pretend this is not the case and try to keep the dream alive for just a few minutes longer.

I reach for her face but like a blind person, she does not flinch. "I fear never being with you."

Her tears are turned to silver in the moonlight. As an image it is achingly beautiful and so dreadfully sad. "I will always be with you. I am part of who you are."

No matter the delusions of recent times, there is no escaping the truth of the moment. "I don't want to go."

She closes her eyes, but the tears will not be trapped by such a device. "Goodbye, my love."

The world about me becomes translucent and the stars bleed through, and I now know I have never had any real choice in the matter. Even in death we are clinging on to each other like survivors gripping driftwood as the Beaufort scale rises.

But I don't want to leave this woman, this place, this connection to the earth and the life I have lived upon it. Yet even as I think such a thing, I feel the story running towards its final few paragraphs, the sentences skimming past my eyes as the cover is about to close.

What then? A quiet contemplation as reader and narrator connect for one final moment, the scale of what has been told and its impact felt, digested? A decision made based on if this was an experience to savour every once in a while, pulled from a shelf, the cover fondly caressed and courted, a good, good memory to relive? Or one for the charity shop, tossed in a box and dumped in the boot of a car, unworthy and meaningless?

My story is ending, and there is the fear that I shall never know the answer. There is a pain in my heart, but like the morphine in the final stages, the agony of the tumours that guzzled on my colon is kept distant, the liquor of begrudging acceptance.

Marianne has gone to the kitchen, collecting her precious book *en route*, and now sits at the table as she begins to wane. She has one hand on her heart, and another placed on the copy of *Wuthering Heights*. I wonder – as I move from one place to another, crossing realms, unimpeded by barrier nor boundary – if I have, for a moment in time at least, become her very own Heathcliff.

The sad smile on her face as I recede tells me, not for the first time in our brief, beautiful life, that we are in tune with the very same thought. It is enough to know I will remain on the bookshelf in her mind, a good memory to pass away a few spare moments. Recollections are the lifeblood of those departed, I knew this edict before my own demise. But the certainty of this ever-present notion – that I am to be kept real and unforgotten — gives me my cue to let go, to accept what I must and leave behind what once was and what I am destined to become: content – embraced and absorbed – diminished yet rewritten by the fabric of the universe.

One day my Marianne will join me, our consciousness becoming one, as our bodies once did back in the realm of the corporeal. This certainty satisfies – calms – and like Heathcliff and Cathy, we shall roam the heavens for eternity. No beginning, no end, just the everlasting *now*.

For we *are* the cosmos.

Dave Jeffery is the author of 18 novels and novellas, two collections, and numerous short stories and essays. His *Necropolis Rising* series and yeti adventure *Frostbite* have both featured on the Amazon #1 bestseller list. His YA work features the Beatrice Beecham supernatural adventures. Jeffery is also the creator of the *A Quiet Apocalypse* series which has received worldwide critical acclaim. Actively involved in the Horror Writers Association (HWA), Jeffery is a mentor on the HWA Mentorship Scheme for which he was a recipient of the Bram Stoker Mentor of the Year Award for 2022, and he is co-chair of the HWA Wellness Committee.

He can be found at: www.davejefferyauthor.com

Steadfast, Before Beast Of Gilded Ruin

by Josh Poole

What figure nestles in the mortal char
Lain cross gilded ruin with ragged pelt
Its mouth blackened, besieged by boiling tar
By which cruel demons' will, its hand been dealt?

Black tongue tethered to throat, it bides penance
No longer to vouchsafe thy cauldron's spark
Old scars, old fates, ordained by rote vengeance
By whose broadsword thy bulwarked hide been marked?

Though bred of thunder, thy are still lizard
Speaketh thee, before thy words go to rot
Was thy snout once tasseled with kings' innards
Have thine deeds of fire been long forgot?

Do I profane you with remembrance?
Or be my words, thy sole inheritance?

Josh Poole is a visual artist and writer born and raised in a sleepy mountain town. His work often depicts the lifestyle and tradition of those who live at the periphery of society through the lens of fantasy parables.

The Bell
by Cecile Llewelyn-Rajan

My lady's hair is wet and heavy. I like to lose my fingers in it, sometimes; snared in her like a fish in a net. Her skin is sunless, so fine her blood vessels make an indigo filigree, and her tail is long and strong as it twists around my legs and pins me close enough against her to feel the thunder of her heart against my own.

Merries, we call her kind here, in the Hundred, which is amusing, because my name is Mererid.

When I was younger, I believed it fate; that we were destined. The Hundred is a flat, treeless plane bridging two vaster cantrefs; we are wholly at the whims of the water. Our ties with the Merries are ancient, and once it was the fashion to name your children *Pearl* or *Sprat*, or plait kelp in your hair and tan fish skin into skirts that skim the sand, a crude mimicry of tails. For longer than anyone living can remember, it has been custom that should the Prince or Princess of the Hundred have issue, the firstborn is wed to the land, while the second is given to the sea, to honour those age-old bonds.

I was born seven minutes after my sister, screaming and purple as she was sweetly serene. I was always thus, I could not help it; combative and quarrelsome to balance her docility—until the day my mother, the Princess of the Hundred, told me I was to be the bride of the sea. I had already met my lady, you see, skipping stones at the shoreline; I had heard her liquid laugh, and touched her silver scales. Her name is not a word of runes or letters, but a *feeling*, and she had taught me it so that I could breathe it in the silence when my sister was asleep; so that I could touch myself and imagine her chill, slippery fingers in place of my own.

It was not a fate I dreaded by any stretch of the imagination.

We have long venerated the waters, you understand. It is the closest thing my people have to a god; it is our livelihood, it is our living; and, like a god, it is as awful as it is generous. The tide is prone to gushing in when it should creep, and it does not adhere to the moon's pattern. Tempests wrack it, riptides swirl invisible patterns beneath the surface, and thus is the Merries' living, to police it, their breathy, eerie music coaxing shoals into fishermen's nets, or mollifying the churn and slap of the water.

But even they have not dominion over the sea, not entirely.

It was summer when the tempest came, so abrupt and so furious that even the Merries could not temper it, however loudly they sang. My mother and sister were on the open water at the time, paying private homage to the sea, as they did every season. I think I was wrestling with a netter's child on the beach when the clouds began to boil and blacken above me as if bruised. I saw the brown freckle of my mother's coracle disappear beneath the prickling waves before a vassal dragged me to safety.

The Merries brought their bodies in the following morning when the storm had subsided somewhat. They did not understand this custom of ours; they were not human, and under their philosophy all the lives the sea claimed replenished those that it did not, but they humoured it anyway, dragging their bodies with gawky care as far up the beach as their tails would let them rove, leaving obscene smears in the sand. My sister's acorn-coloured skin was ashen, my mother's fine-boned face lumpy with death bloat. My lady was there, just beyond the shoreline, her lovely silver eyes shut in sympathy, or her version thereof. It was then, I think, that my father decided to hate the Merries, for he had never had a strong opinion about anything before my mother died. I can remember acutely watching his black eyes grow blacker still as he looked upon the mer-people, and saw all about them that was other.

It was chilling.

There was no longer any question of my marriage to the sea. I would have fought, had I any sense beyond the appalling enormity that my twin sister was already carrion. I was a bit obsessed with that, actually; I spent days looking at the patch of sand where she had lain, imagining that I could still see her outline whatever the tide's sluicing. I did not notice when the castle began to fill with men, their grave, rumbly voices echoing around the cobwebby rafters.

Not until my father bade me dress in my finest frock, of forest-green velvet, and attend him.

"I have called you here," he said, and the feasting cacophony hushed around him, as though he was someone who mattered. His voice had always been reedy, better suited to sweet nothings and muttered niceties than oration, and sounded shrill to my ears. "I have called you all here," he said again, "because I have come to a decision. For too long the Hundred has been a slave to the sea, and all therein. We have no trees to defend us from its storms, no reef to break the fury of the tide. And as for the Merries—" he filled his chest, a bird-like mockery of potency, and yet potent for all that, "there is nothing *merry* about them. They are *monstrosities*, fish with fingers, faces. Demons, surely, or something of that ilk. It is not for goodly folk to venerate them."

My grief was like a wet wool cloak, deadening me to the world; it took a long moment for his words to take effect.

"But Da," I said eventually. "The Merries are not our enemies, for goodness' sake! You said yourself not a few weeks since that without them we would be defenceless against the sea."

"Forgive my daughter," he said to the hall. "She is grieving; she does not mean to be so obdurate. But I suppose you are right, child. Indeed, is not this tragedy proof that what we need most of all is a proper defence against the waters? And so do I mean to build a dyke, all along the entire seaward border of the Hundred, with a great bell atop its crown to frighten the Merries away. Not only will it protect us from the waves, and all therein, so will it make us rich besides, for with it we and we alone shall police what trade passes through these waters, and in doing so, fill our fief's coffers fit to bursting!"

I felt like I had fallen into a looking glass, that everything was familiar and yet subtly, disgustingly wrong. Were my mother here, she would have calmed them, she would have made them see reason. Were my sister, she would have danced or done something else decorous - something to distract away from their cankerous thoughts. But there was just me, and this man who once was my father, though I could not have recognised him less.

I daresay my father expected me to protest because he grabbed my nape, and, as I cringed, hauled me from the great hall, tangling me up in my own train.

"You will be silent," he commanded, smashing me against the wall. I am tall, and the curlicue of a sconce dug into my spinal column. "As your sister was when she knew it was in her best interest."

"I do not care about *my* best interest," I replied. "I care about what is in the *Hundred's* best interest. What kind of fool are you to cut all ties with the sea? You cannot believe that Mam would have sanctioned this! There is no wisdom here!"

"But there is justice." And I saw then that his eyes were so full of hate as though even the pattern of his irises was spikes, but something worse, too, something closer to calculation. "I cannot castigate the sea for killing my lady, my daughter. But I can keep it from claiming anyone else, and, more than that, I can see the Hundred profit from this tragedy."

My belly moiled as though I had eaten dirty slush. "But what of *my* lady, da? You would sever me from the sea to which I have been promised for my life entire?"

It was the wrong thing to say; something I have a talent for. But I had not learned, not yet, the trick of dishonesty. Before my eyes, any residual warmth he had once felt for me fled him. "You will wed a good *human* lad, child, under whose guidance you will rule the Hundred. The sea has claimed enough of mine already."

"But the Merries—"

"*Do not speak that word to me again.*"

I should have fought him. I should have refused. Even my pacific sister would have argued with him against this profanity. But shock and grief rendered me stupid, and so I dumbly let his vassals return me to my chamber.

I rue it now though, as I curl atop my pallet, and think about my lady.

Think about the way her second eyelids close when she is lost in the rapture of climax, think about her scales, rough and slippery between my thighs. I grieve her like she is dead, but she is not dead, I can hear her singing to the squalls, singing to the riptides; one voice amongst many otherworldly voices, only hers to me is clear as ringing steel.

And then I hear, over the Merries' singing, the pulse of masons' picks, and the wheeze of saw against wood. I rise from my bed-furs and watch through a crack in the grouting as my father's builders begin his dyke, dust clouds a sick margin all around the Hundred. My heart is surely made of the self-same quarried stone.

Mother, I think. *What would you do if you could see your cantref now?*

But I know what she would do. She would stop it, by any means necessary.

And so must I.

It does not work.

I escape my chamber when the castle is asleep, I hack at the stones with my mother's sword before the mortar has begun to set. My father hears me, sends vassals to pen me in my room. I stop eating out of protest; the servants force open my jaw and siphon mashed fare down my gullet until I nearly breathe it until I have no choice but to swallow or else drown. I piss through my wears, I pull hanks of hair from my scalp, I bite and kick and scratch anyone who dares minister to me, but that serves only to poison my cause, and me, too, in their eyes. Then I appeal to them, pathetically obsequious even to my ears; I remind them of the festivals we have shared with the Merries, how the very fish they break their fast on will be lost to them, how they cannot imprison the sea. I can hear the Merries wauling in rage and grief that my father has forsaken the bonds our people have long sworn to theirs; that they have been denied me, the bride of the sea, and I tell the servants this, too, and make them listen with me.

But I might be waves roaring against some distant shore, so little do they heed me. "Listen to your father, child," they tell me, those few who deign to acknowledge I exist. "The Prince knows what is best for us all."

And he loves it, this newfound respect the common folk have for him. No longer is he the bumbling, foolish husband of the Princess. When he enters the great hall — for he still forces me to feast with him however I abuse myself; he dams my intransigence with a stubbornness I did not know he possessed — folk fawn flusteredly and mutter breathlessly amongst themselves, as though he were twice as tall and half again as broad across the chest. I hate him, I think, I hate him so much that my guts tangle like old trawl, but I cannot help admiring how deftly he has made of this tragedy a whetstone, honing him into something more dynamic than even my mother had been.

He frightens me, in truth. When his eyes spear towards mine, I cannot hold them for long.

"...and so it is with enormous pleasure that I can announce," he is saying, something about his hateful wall, and I am only half listening. (The lord beside me has breath like decaying flowers; I wonder if I make myself sick, will my father force me to endure another of these interminable feasts). He has struggled of late to find the means with which to build a sluice, to let in the low tide and bar the high, without creating a flaw that some water-borne assault could later exploit, "- that I can announce," my father continues, "that while building, a rare talent was found amidst the masons. Seith, lad, step forward now. Come here, show these good folk what you can do."

The boy is pretty, his skin the deep, nutty tan native to the Hundred, and his eyes large, warming yellow-green. I watch him absently, then with intent as I take note of the way he moves. It is awkward, tentative, as if his feet alone might shatter the very earth he treads. He looks around the room, aghast at the attention, and then his eyes come to rest on me. I have not my sister's perception or attention span; at another time, I would not have noticed the determination sharpening his jawline, the thrill sparking in his gaze, but now I have nothing else to do but watch.

And he wants me to.

With more confidence now, he takes from his pocket a black rock, the size of a human heart. He passes it across the hall. Anyone yet feasting or conversing falls silent, examining the stone. When it is my turn, I can feel my father's eyes intent as two primed arrows upon my face. In full view of him, the hall and this Seith too, I raise the stone before me, then drop it with provocative force to the rushes. I want it to crumble or crack, but Hundred stone is as adamantine, and can be broken only by itself.

Still, it displeases my father, which pleases me.

If Seith is daunted or upset, there is no sign of it in his face. Impassively, he recovers the rock, his braecs creaking in the riveted silence, and proffers it between his thumb and finger. He stares at it for a tedious moment, and then prises his fingers from its juts. It does not drop.

It does not drop.

It is a tiny moon, hovering before him, and my heart is cantering, cantering. *Witch*, it tells me; *witch, witch, witch.*

A witch has not been seen in the Hundred in centuries. In the old legends, that tell of when the first settlers came to these planes and made enemies of the Merries with their greed and careless ravening of the waters, it was a witch who forged the peace upon which the Hundred has thrived ever since.

I sit on the very brink of my throne.

Seith frowns at the rock, and now as I watch it divides itself, an organic tear along its jagged grain, weeping little streams of dust. Awe susurrates across the room; my father smiles like a cat with a rat. Somewhat self-consciously, Seith wills the cleave together again, the stone teeming and mutating like something sort of living under his cajoling, then returns it to me.

It is not as it was before. Now it is shaped like a fish-tail in motion, cobbled all over in tiny, delicate scales no larger than grains of sand.

He mocks me, this Seith; he seeks to remind me of all I have lost.

I feel every drop of blood flee my face.

"So you see," says my father, giving Seith a paternal slap on the shoulder, "now we have a witch at our disposal, we need not concern ourselves with building a sluice. Indeed, any shipborne trade that dares people these waters will be ours to govern, for none can pass our great levee without Seith's permission. He shall be our living sluice, our Master of the Waves, and we, my good people, will be rich!"

And as he speaks, he looks at me, and the triumph in his eyes makes me feel sick.

I peel away. They will notice I am missing soon enough, and probably I should put this reprieve to some use, but I take myself to my father's wall instead. It is almost entirely built now; a fringe of loveless black. I can hear the tide rising sibilantly behind it. I scale a crenellation, let the wind lash at my hair, bawling hysterically around me.

"*Don't!*" says a voice behind me.

I do not intend to jump — I have considered it and have come to the chilly conclusion that I would better spite my father to live, a thorn in his side — but unsolicited, a pair of knuckly hands haul me awkwardly backwards. Seith pants beside me on the walkway, his gaze so wide I can map the tree-root blood vessels bordering his eyes.

"Why?" I demand. "Why save me, if I did mean to jump? Would not it please you, to be rid of me?"

I've shocked him. I often shock people, but he is bloodless.

"My lady, no," and the words are nearly matter, taking little chunks of him with them. "I could not want that less."

It takes me a moment to understand.

"You love me," I say tonelessly.

It is lovely, the glossy lustre his eyes take on. The stone, I realise, was not a mockery at all, but a token of his esteem.

"Why?"

He barks a shaky laugh. He is younger than me, I reckon. "Why does the land love the sea? Because it is lovely and unbending. Because it has depths far beyond the knowledge of men and women. Because it is most beautiful of all when it rages, and you, my lady Mererid, are always raging."

He fathoms himself a poet, this Seith. My face warms and I hate myself for it.

"Yet you would try to stem its flow? You would be this — what was it my father called you, *Master of the Waters*?"

"Of the Waves," he corrects me apologetically. "And as for that, I do as my Prince bids me, no more or less."

"Why? What does he offer you in return?"

It cannot merely be land or prosperity; a witch has access to all that in any cantref they choose to root themselves. No, it has to be something he *really* wants, to keep him in the Hundred.

Slowly, Seith looks at me. And with that look, any melancholy that had made a home in me falls away like so many cobwebs.

"Oh, you poor, sweet boy," I say. "You think he will give you *me*, don't you?"

He does not speak, his flush so furious I can feel the heat rolling off it, and retreats from the parapet before I have a chance to tease him.

It doesn't matter. I know, at last, what I must do.

I change nothing of my behaviour. My father would know I was preoccupied; he is altogether cannier than I ever could have reckoned, so I am as revolting and obstinate as I have always been, if not worse. The servants do not even try to dress or feed me now, so many scars have I left upon them, but piss in the water they leave me to wash in and hide roaches in my bed-furs.

I do not care. I watch through the break in the grouting as the dyke is built, and the bell is craned in to crown it. It is a brass monstrosity, its girth as large if not larger still than me from brow to foot, clanging a bleak rhythm as it is even fixed into place.

I can no longer hear the Merries. Some days I am not sure I did not imagine them altogether.

The bell rings day and night, relentless and pervasive. It vibrates my bed-furs, my blood, I can feel it like tooth-rot in my jaw, my joints. I wonder if anyone else hears it, that they can so blithely and so selfishly continue their lives despite its deafening boom.

I wonder if I am going mad.

A spike of sunlight snags on the hairs I tore from my scalp some days since. I collect them together, card out the knots and then begin to braid them, a long black rope like a sea serpent.

When the dyke is finished my father calls for a feast and invites all the princes and princesses from all the neighbouring cantrefs. He dresses me in a frock of cloth of silver, braiding what is left of my hair as gently and meticulously as he once did in my youth, proud if not of me then of this new Hundred he has created, and the role I will play in it. I think he expects me to fight him, but all the while I am stiff as stone, anticipation welling at my armpits. I panic that he can smell it, that he can read my thoughts as though my skull has turned to water, but he just smiles, folds my hand in the crook of his elbow, and leads me down to the great hall.

The festival is manic, almost raucous enough to overwhelm the bell's pealing. Gone is the salty tang of fresh, fried fish and the sharp, brackish fumes of steamed seaweed; now these seafaring folk feast on imported fowl and cereals from far-off lands, boiled until inedible because our cooks know not what to do with them. My father gets drunk, because he can, because his dyke is finished and my mother and sister are avenged, and keeps my goblet tremulously full. I drink too, because I might as well, though I can taste nothing but salt and ashes.

Then he leads us to the parapet, to watch Seith — decked in a new, sealy doublet with silver beads weighing down his hair — split the very wall itself in two as though it was made of cotton roving, letting in the low tide and any trade who would curry favour here. It is extraordinary, even my breath clots in my throat, but as I peer over the parapet, I fancy I can see the sparkling suggestion of silver scales beneath the water.

My father watches me.

"And what about when the tide comes in?" I ask him without inflection, or seeming interest. 'For we all know of the fury of the rising tide. What will you do then, father?"

My father gives me a look of irritation. "Then Seith shall sew the levee back together again."

I wait.

It requires discipline beyond anything I've ever known to keep my expression bored and impassive. My father takes a woman to his lap, lets her mouth his throat and fondle beneath his doublet as though my mother did not occupy that very throne a month since, and watches me all the while.

He does it to make me hate him, I think; he does it because he has mistaken fear for power, and folk take his example. They hiss execrable names in my direction, throw little gobbets of food into my hair. They feast and fight and make of this hallowed hall an orgy, and do not notice when I slip away to the parapet.

The bell is so loud here that I breathe its grim rhythm. The moon paints the feathering muscles of Seith's back silver, making a nimbus of his hair as he turns to face me.

"My lady," he says, and in his mouth, my voice is a poem. But then he frowns. "You cannot be here. The tide is coming in. You will — I need to — "

I silence him with my mouth. He tastes wrong, too sweet, too warm, his lips soft as a bog. I try to remember my lady's mouth, salty and salubriously cool, but I cannot, not really, not enough.

"Mererid," he groans into my mouth as he paws me through the rustling cloth of silver. His desire is shocking in its clumsy insistence, I can hardly breathe for the oniony entitlement of his sweat, and yet I let him reach for me and reach for him in return, and pretend I am enjoying it, pretend I can feel anything at all except the bell throbbing above us.

And slowly, slowly, the tide unfurls, cunning as I am. It chews at the beach, the breakwater, chomps down the cobblestones branching between the cottages. It is our god, endless and inexorable, sluicing the Hundred clean.

And everyone will drown in its embrace.

My father does not notice. He revels still in the great hall, stupid in his arrogance as the tide insidiously dampens the rushes, laps warmly at his clogs, and I am glad, I am glad. Higher and higher it rises, swirling and sloshing inside the little bothies, spewing from their mouths like blood from open wounds. Even when the children begin to scream, when I see the bodies rising to the surface of the waves, I am glad, a villain in earnest.

I am the bride of the sea, and to the sea, I give these spoils.

It takes Seith a moment to realise what we have done. The waves glitter on either side of the parapet now, filtering over the troughs.

"Mererid," he gasps. *"What have you done?"*

He does not expect an answer, and I do not give it. He wades away from me, reaching inwardly for whatever metaphysical matter it is that makes his magic, and I hear the rock rumble with his mastering. It cannot be borne. From my sleeve, I take the thick braid and garrotte him with it. He squirms and gargles, long legs kicking wildly at the water pooling on the walkway, his clever hands scrabbling flyaways from the tightly-plaited hair, but I am stronger than I seem, and I can hear my lady singing my name.

I come, my love, I reply, *my lady, I come.*

Seith falls limp against my legs. If he is not yet dead, it doesn't matter; he will be shortly. The water is at my waist now, a chill girdle, prickling breasts, my clavicle; soon it will carry me away with it.

In the end, it is a relief when the water closes over my head like a careful, consoling mouth.

Even here, I hear the bell, tolling with the current, but now it sounds dull and indistinct. I drift, weightless in the blue, airlessness making comets of my vision, until my fingers tangle in something like hair, and something scaled coils around my ankle. Saltwater burns my eyes when I open them, but it doesn't matter, it doesn't matter.

For here is my lady, my love, and her lips are parting for a kiss.

With the incisive prose and imagery of Madeleine Miller's *Galatea* and Celtic atmosphere of *The Mists of Avalon*, *The Bell* is a 4,500 word fantasy retelling of the old Welsh legend of Cantre'r Gwaelod — known by some as the Welsh Atlantis. I am a mum of two and makeup artist based in the Cotswolds, UK. When not writing or doing other people's makeup, I am usually found cooking something unnecessarily complicated, folding laundry or reheating lukewarm cups of tea.

Deforestation

by Emma Gritt

'It's not called tree hugging now, the term's forest bathing.'
She said pointing at the ramblers, 'it's trendy not crazy.
'You absorb strength and wisdom from the trunk and roots.
Ask it questions and thank it, it does you good!'
Have you ever wondered how the earth's got much busier?
Like locusts, destroying green spaces, ancient reincarnation sums are obliterated.
But what if this influx, of people fuelled by evil, cruelty and greed,
Are vessels for the devilish souls who were once trapped in trees?
With some monster arbors hundreds of years old
They might once have been a criminal who would make your blood run cold.
That looming oak on the hill, was once a woman feted by her village
Until she killed her baby, her husband, neighbour and dog.
She seduced and killed a priest, then drank his blood.
The universe decreed her punishment was to spend her next life standing alone and naked in mud.
Beautiful once, now gnarled and creaking, pissed on by men and dogs, her bark scratched at by children.
1,000 years should have been long enough to ponder her deeds —
But her sentence was cut short by a chainsaw, and she was set free.
Now her soul's in your newborn child. There's a glint in its eye, the baby's not right.
It cries, bites and wails, gnaws on its crib and refuses to sleep.

Wait til you see what he grows in to. A murderer, thief and perverse voyeur.
You'll blame yourself, but it's all down to her.
We've all heard the whispers and sighs amongst the trees
But what are they really saying, to you and to me?
I once hugged a tree and it told me to kill.
I went back to my village and slew all my kin.
Now it's me standing still for 500 years.
I'm not sorry for my actions I'd do it again.
And trust me, I will, once this timber is felled.

Emma Gritt is half-way through writing a novel, and spends most of her free time tending to (i.e. cleaning up after) her Romanian rescue cats, Dennis and Burny. Her aim for 2023? Learn how to make risotto, and watch every episode of *Tales Of The Unexpected*.

Ida
by Teika Marija Smits

As usual, I find myself staring at the woman in the painting, 'Interior' by Vilhelm Hammershøi. I cannot see her face – she has her back to the viewer – and as usual, I wonder what she looks like from the front.

It is early morning and there are few visitors to the National Gallery. No one intrudes on my reverie – no one breaks the spell the woman has cast over me. I wonder what she was thinking when the painter trapped her in this moment forever, in the austere room with its grey walls and wan light. It is obvious that the painter – a he, of course, aren't they all? (look around, there are no she-artists in the gallery) – was inspired by Vermeer. The colours are mournful, the woman's black dress pitiful. The woman is nothing more than an object which has been appropriately placed, studied, and then rendered realistically. The woman is also the painter's wife. Her name is Ida.

What would Ida have said if she were allowed her own voice? Perhaps she was weary of being her husband's model. Perhaps she longed to hold a brush and palette and to paint pictures herself. Or perhaps the black gown is an outward sign of a pious soul who found solace in the rituals of religion. Or maybe it tells us of a secret grief – a lost child, a heart bruised for evermore.

Then again, I reflect that the artist, the husband, may have done Ida no disservice. Perhaps they lived in comfortable domesticity, and Ida felt fulfilled by her role as wife and muse and keeper of the household. Perhaps Vilhelm was faithful to her, unlike so many husbands. Perhaps she was a modestly attractive woman and so her life was tolerable, for well do I know that us women live by our faces. Even if we are in possession

42

of a fortune, or a sparkling wit, or a clever mind, it matters not, if our face does not please. My daughter, poor soul, her face scarred by a violent dog, thought herself unfit to marry. And now, wise with age, I truly understand what it means to be judged by one's face. Once, I was called beautiful. But to those who come to visit me now, I am the ugly, titled woman. No one remembers the things I did when I was young. No one remembers that I used to be a passionate advocate for musicians and writers.

I wonder, for what must be the thousandth time, what it is that Ida is holding, for surely the object in her hands must be a vital clue to her story. Is it a letter from a friend – a fellow housewife, perhaps – who writes about the latest fashion in table linens and the price of herring? Or could it be something far more intimate – a letter, maybe, from a man who once admired Ida but didn't dare to declare himself? A man who longs to embrace her. But perhaps she holds only a list of items that she intends to buy when she goes to market.

Yet it is true, as some of the other admirers of Ida have said, that silence emanates from the painting like a fog that has rolled out from the river and flooded the city streets with an eerie stillness. Mostly, I am comforted by this silence, but sometimes I am frightened by it. But perhaps I am being melodramatic. Perhaps Ida and Vilhelm were loving spouses. Then I can imagine the silence as a comfortable almost-pause, an enjambment between lines in a stanza of a poem about love. But at other times, when I fancy that the air grows chill in the gallery, I am certain that the silence is a tension, a violin string about to break, and that Ida will snap at any moment, her restrained emotions bursting forth. It is then that I want to scream, *Get out, Ida, get out!* For I know all too well what it is to be trapped.

Amid these ruminations, I hear approaching steps. A man and woman enter the room Ida and I are in and tour the room disinterestedly. I assume they are a couple – they have that horrid and modern familiarity with each other – and though at first, they walk straight past me, oblivious, before they leave the room they pause beside me.

"Princess Pauline Metternich," says the woman loudly, as though I am deaf, as well as dumb.

Ida's true narrative, which I so nearly grasped as it unfurled like a fern from the canvas, is now gone. My eyes glaze over, and I re-fix myself in daubs of paint, revert to pigment and old, old oil.

"Degas, apparently," says the man. "Though you wouldn't know it. Would you?"

I wonder at their stupidity, their need to state the obvious as they look up at me vacantly.

"Not one of his best," adds the woman.

"No," agrees the man. "She's no great beauty."

They stare at me for a little while longer, and then move on to take a closer look at 'The Two Friends' by Toulouse-Lautrec before they leave the room I am hanging in. They never said anything about Ida, either bad or good, and this, for some reason, makes me glad. She is *my* secret to uncover.

Teika Marija Smits is a UK-based writer and freelance editor. She writes poetry and fiction, and her speculative short stories have been published in *Parsec, Best of British Science Fiction* and *Great British Horror 6*. She is delighted by the fact that Teika means fairy tale in Latvian. https://teikamarijasmits.com/

Outside The Falling Magnolia Petals
by Tricia Lloyd Waller

Tormented twins standing serenely
either side of the store cupboard door.
Smoke spiralling gently through
the twisted and tarnished keyhole.
But still they stand like identical statues
smote from but one slab of ice.

Whilst outside the falling magnolia petals
begin to cover the withered remains of
their marmalade tabby kitten who
used to lap chocolate flavoured milk from
their bone china Tabitha Twitchit bowls.

Tricia Lloyd Waller has always loved story since she first learnt to speak. She has recently had work accepted by *The Poet, Wildfire Words* and *Candlelit* magazine. She was last year's winner of *The Pen to Print* poetry competition.

Munro Baggers
by Finola Scott

The moon and her companions have not long left the sky and the humming birds are back, clamouring. Greedy buggers, such show-offs. Humming birds so far north now. Shouldn't be surprised. Birds from the tales all gone. Sparrows, curlews replaced with those who bask in the heat of the Warming. These pirouetting drug addicts crave sugar, more sugar, like playground tots of old. Little razor teeth, rainbow hued, saw-rasped. That gutsy tongue lapping like a bar-room gigolo. Their tiny teeth will rot. Teeth? Did birds always have teeth?

Everything has changed, the Warming hasn't only affected the creatures. There have been so many consequences. I am proud of how well this group manages it all. We've routines, discussions as equals. They do look to me, but that's ok. My grandparents, great-grandparents passed down so much information. I know about handlooms and farming using the moon's phases to maximise crops. I'm no clan chief, just someone who wants to survive and not to be alone. I have to admit the work load is heavy.

The pool's disappeared again. Must be something dead somewhere blocking the flow in the canal. Another elk no doubt. We daren't be water short like those down south where Mother Earth's tit is sucked dry. Here we feel blessed with solid dry land as well as fresh water, although we must keep vigilant to maintain the flow. We need to watch for lizards clawing their way up our banks. Time to time they flick their tails in thirst-anger, insist on more water. Pee's no substitute. Anyway the mills need it more. Or the Weaving. The children keep growing and new clothes are needed – again!

Soon the Group will arrive to waulk the bark-cloth. Who would have thought the Warming would bring old skills, new songs and re-find the Gaelic? A lot of work but wonderful to see bark turned to garments. What else needs done this week? I must check the farming charts as harvest time nears. The sickle moon phase is best. Sickles, oh the swish sweep slicing of crops in the Amber ripening time. And the moon so steadfast through it all. I watch it wax and wane. Ever ripe and ready.

Our moon has seen it all afore – the ice melting, the land heaving, shifting, throwing up our mountains. She tide-hauls oceans, washes shores, snatches cliffs from land's edges. Oh she has powers. We must remember that, we must always pay heed, learn from the past.

First, I need to organise a squad to reinforce the ramparts. Scattered gunfire approaches. The Watchers posted on the crags will alert us at any shadows. Southern gangs are creeping near, we know. The panels of the cars are peeling. Windscreens falling out. Rubber tyres long gone for shoes. Cars were never meant as walls. But how solid our Car-henges are, how much they have withstood.

I remember cars in old films, in fiches. People driving across the country to watch moon launches. What a notion! Sending a big metal box into the sky, right up as far as they can? Why? The moon wasn't meant to be sullied, trod on, just another place to conquer. Can't be true. But if it is, maybe that's what caused the Disturbance, caused the Ice Melt, the woods to burn. Interfering with the Firmament. No. They'd not be so daft to do that. It must be a story for bed-time bairns.

That's enough day-dreaming! I've responsibilities. That gun fire still approaches, cloud rattling. These marauders must be metal rich, fuel poor. They snake near on empty bellies, greedy for our peat and peaks. Too close now. Last night the noise was persistent like the clatter of pebbles on midnight roofs. Distant anger punctures our dreams, dims our candles.

Must be a large group. They shall not bag our Munros.

Finola Scott's work is scattered on the wind, on posters, tapestries. It is published in *Shoreline of Infinity*, *Gutter* and *New Writing Scotland*. Red Squirrel Press publish her pamphlet *Much left unsaid*. Dreich publish *Count the ways*. Tapsalteerie publish her latest work *Modren Makars: Yin*.

Clio's Revenge

by David C. Kopaska-Merkel

It wasn't enough that I was saddled
with responsibility for history,
a subject no one ever got right
(few tried; so many axes to grind),
or that Aphrodite made me crush
on that male chauvinist king
(at least he was mortal, thank Zeus;
I was released from servitude,
eventually, by his death).

No, I finally get a bit of respect,
a street is named after me,
and because the City of New Orleans,
in its infinite wisdom,
uses a sans-cerif font on street signs,
the locals call MY street "C-L fucking 10!"
Tourists think it's funny,
but if they knew history,
they'd know that mocking a
titan like myself has consequences.
A storm is just what's needed;
Poseidon is missing in action,
but, on Athena's sisterly advice,
I've been suppressing climate-

48

change warnings for generations.
The city's been lucky so far,
but the Big One is coming.
I'll be laughing last and loudest
when the Big Easy ends up on the bottom
of Lake Pontchartrain.

David C. Kopaska-Merkel has been writing speculative poetry and fiction since the 1970s. He won the 2006 Rhysling award for best long poem (for a collaboration with Kendall Evans), and edits *Dreams & Nightmares* magazine (since 1986). He has edited *Star*line*, an issue of *Eye To The Telescope*, and several *Rhysling* anthologies, has served as SFPA president, and is an SFPA Grandmaster. His poems (more than 1200 of them) have been published in *Asimov's, Strange Horizons,* and more than 200 other venues. *Some Disassembly Required*, his latest collection of dark poetry, was published by Diminuendo Press in 2022. @DavidKMresists on CS.
Blog: https://dreamsandnightmaresmagazine.blogspot.com/

Imperatrix
by Nemma Wollenfang

"So," said Daire, as he swirled the amber brew in his allo-mech flagon, "you want someone dead."

There was only one reason the old coot had the gall to approach him in the space-station's seedy little tavern, despite the dire warnings from the cyborg barkeep to steer clear. It was because he needed a job done. And everyone knew Daire was the best at what he did. No bragging, just unassailable fact. Who else had a hit rate like his? Nobody. That's why his name was feared and admired in equal measure, all across the galaxy. That's why he boasted a kill count of five-and-sixty. And if another began to encroach on that, well... he made sure to eliminate the competition. Adding to his score.

"They... they say you're the one to talk to about such." The fancy gent looked well out of place in the *Android's Arm*, what with his plush brocade and neatly combed snowy hair. All soft skin and not a callus on him. The lack of engine oil said a lot too. *An imperial colonist.* Folk like him rarely ventured this far out into the boondocks, unless they were desperate.

A brawny deckhand with an infra-red optic and bulky mechno-arm brushed past then, sloshing his brew with a gruff "*Watch it*", and the pretentious codger visibly quaked in his soft suede shoes, the navy striations across his face dimming like a whipped whelp's. Pitiful.

"My services are costly, Grandfather. For what I do, I charge a great deal." Even then he was very selective about his clientele, about which jobs he took. But this man... the aroma of wealth hung about him, the fine stitch of his clothes seeped money. He smelt sweet, looked clean. All while loitering in a sticky hovel that stunk of iron rot. For him, coin would be no issue.

As if to confirm that thought, the aged fellow tossed a pouch onto the table with a thud.

"Would this be sufficient?"

It looked to be a hefty sum, at least two thou. How it had not been pilfered by the many urchins running rampant through this space station's docks he'd never know.

Daire didn't let his surprise show, didn't so much as twitch towards the pouch. Instead, he eyed the dregs in his flagon, letting disinterest shine through. A callous and cool mien.

"There's another waiting, upon completion of the job," the gent hurried on, sweat beading on his brow. He dabbed at it with a silk kerchief, loosing a 'squeak' at the clatter of allo-mech that preceded the breakout of a brawl in the far corner. "Ten thou draknars in total," he gulped as two deckhands crashed into a table, "with compliments from the one I represent."

Ah, so this was just the middleman, a petty mediary. The client likely sought anonymity, didn't want anything to lead back to them. Not unusual. That, or they felt the task of acquiring Daire's services to be beneath them. Whatever the reason, Daire had ways of uncovering his employers' identities, of ripping away their masks. He'd find them out, he always did.

Taking one last swig, he set down the flagon, finally giving the man his full focus. "And the name of the target?" Which – likely undeserving – fool was to be the lamb to slaughter?

From the pocket of his frockcoat, the man retrieved a crumpled piece of paper and, after checking over both shoulders, set it before Daire on the scarred, metallic table top.

Daire went rod straight, tense as iron cable. His striations flared blue.

"Is there a problem?" The gent's eyes narrowed, crinkling with crow's feet.

Finally, slowly, Daire leaned forward, weighing the pouch in his grasp.

"Ten thou draknars, you say?" He loosed a low laugh. "For this particular name, I would've done it for five."

Because that name... it was the one he'd been waiting for.

The target was in the Dynastic System, on the galaxy's outer spiral.

Once the contract was signed and sealed, instructions and payment delivered, Daire was on his way. He travelled hard to get there, to make it in time. Taking the first ship out to the imperial capital of Yii – a class 5 refuse junker, the best to be found on such short notice. Every second of that voyage grated. Sequestered in its cargo hold, he sharpened blades, buffed scopes, tipped darts. Anything to stay the ennui and try to ignore the overwhelming stench of rusting metal. It was best to keep them at the ready anyway. He never knew which he'd need.

Upon arrival, he set up on high ground. A shining sky-tower of glass and steel, set in the centre of the retail sector. Prime location. Perfect, actually. Wetting a finger to test the breeze – low today, minimal drag – he set the sniper on the street below. That steel sang whenever he sent it hurtling through the air – to puncture hide or skin or fibrous membrane. Boasting an unblemished record. That was why all the big shots called him, those with the deepest pockets. They knew he'd get the job done. They trusted him to.

Not that I do this for them.

The festivities were already in full swing. Barrels had been tapped; heady wines flowed, liberally swilled. Folk glutted on rounded rice-cakes – excess the order of the day. Confetti rained down while draconic streamers fluttered; the streets were festooned with ornate lanterns and the high chime of Yii's iconic music mingled with the singing and laughter and cheering of the merrymakers. It was the first time this century that a new ruler would be crowned, and the coronation ceremony had drawn citizens from all corners of the empire.

Testing the lens, Daire spied the length of the thoroughfare. Wings, mandibles, mechs – people from all walks of society were present. The crowds were thick and growing more so by the minute; with the celebrations it was to be expected. He could work with that. Keep a nil on civilian casualties. The target wasn't there, though. Not yet. But they would be, soon.

Hours passed. Time ticked on. Daire's gaze never strayed from the bustling street.

Then... with a blare of trumpets, some artificially magnified voice announced, "Her Imperial Majesty, Pre-Empress Ataraxia the Third!"

And there she was. His assigned quarry. Right there, in his sights. Strolling up onto a magnetically suspended dais in all of her regal splendour, with a trail of courtiers, guards and officials in tow.

Daire adjusted the magnification, increased clarity.

Dark, lustrous hair. Statuesque form. Narrow facial striations of the most delicate azure blue. A regal beauty with a face that could have been hewn from granite. Hard, unforgiving. Power personified. *Just like I remember*... time slowed and warped, memories unravelling.

A child of eight, he'd crept to the palace gates, belly hollow and aching. The royals had been in the midst of a garden party. All that food – too much for those present – had made his stomach keen. Then *she'd* approached. "Why are you here, urchin?" For a solid minute he'd gaped, awed to behold such a striking vision, yet she'd been little more than a child herself. Never before had he seen anyone so neat and clean, so well groomed. With not a hair out of place. "A-a loaf o' bread," he'd finally rasped. "Please... just one loaf." Surely she could spare that much? Lips thin with disdain, she'd summoned a guard.

Doggedly sparring in the training yard, hand to hand with one of the larger cadets, sixteen-year-old Daire strove to win. Failure was not an option. Becoming a Guardsman meant everything. Food, a cosy cot, decent coin. Rain lashed down, blindingly hard, pelleting his bare chest with stinging bullets and making a quagmire beneath his feet. One ill-planned move saw him felled, with a mouthful of blood and filth. Wiping away the mud, he'd found himself at her feet. She looked down. Haughty and disdainful. Imperious and cold. "You fell, boy..."

Upon his induction to the Soldiers' Core, he'd stood in line with the rest of his comrades waiting to receive his graduation medal – a necessary honour for any hoping to earn a position guarding their majesties. None could apply without one. The then-princess had paused before him, regarding him with cool reserve as tendrils of her ebony hair caught in the breeze and his golden medal dangled from her hand. Then, *bypassing* him, she'd said, "Not for you."

Three cutting words that had led him to his current commission. Here and now.

She was the reason he'd worked so hard, risen so high. All for this. This moment. For everything Her Imperial Highness had done, for everything she may yet do... he sighed. The Great Spiralling Cosmos could have that ten thou draknars, he would gladly have worked this assignment for free. Lining his sights, he listened as the crowds fell silent, as the bishuup declared her their new sovereign, setting the gleaming crown atop her head. Sunlight limned each point with sparks of white gold, creating a prismatic dance meant to dazzle all onlookers.

The client was not far away. They never were. They liked to see the job done, their enemies fall. And this one in particular... well, they were the bloodthirsty sort. Vengeful.

He'd glance around to check, but that would mean losing eyes on the target. And he didn't mean to do that, even for a heartbeat.

Breathing deep, he caressed the trigger. Finger firm, bracing for recoil.

The bishuup stepped back.

There. The perfect shot.

Something must have alerted her – reflected sun, a flash of steel, instinct – because the empress turned and there, centre-vision, with scarlet crosshairs marking her face, she stared...

Straight at him.

Those eyes possessed the power to make legions quake. Hot and cold. Fire and stone. She levelled him with a look of pure unyielding flame, knowing what he was and yet utterly fearless. How singular – someone who could look Death in the face and yet not flinch.

No lamb to the slaughter. Ataraxia was more akin to a wolf.

The wind shifted and he adjusted a degree to compensate. There she remained. Not even trying to run. *Because she knows.* She knew he'd return for her in time. She didn't even close her eyes. In fact, as if to challenge him, she raised her imperial chin.

"Defiant to the end," he whispered, squeezing the trigger.

The shot flew. Quick and lethal. One hot streak of metal death that... slammed into the empress's chest with a 'thunk!'

She collapsed like a marionette with its strings cut.

A moment of utter silence. Then...

Chaos.

People screamed. Running, unfurling wings to take to the skies, shifting colour to merge with surrounding buildings.

Blood pooled as Her Majesty's sister dropped to her knees, screaming. The guards rallied then – too late – staffs poised against the unknown threat, eyes darting, striations flaring, while the princess tried to cradle her fallen sibling with shaky, red-stained hands.

"No! Tara! *Noo!*"

Daire smiled, packing away his rifle, knowing he'd not only accomplished his aim but accomplished it *well*. At least, this stage...

A knocked-out guard and a pilfered uniform made it easy to blend seamlessly with the palace staff – who were in such a state of disarray they failed to notice the stranger in their midst. If any had, the weapons Daire sported – gleaming, wicked, displayed just so – were enough to cow most men. Following the trail of blood, he found himself facing the vast steel panels of the throne room. Guards milled about outside, conversing in frantic whispers, while an advisor consoled the weeping princess – who clutched her sister's crown like a talisman.

"I'm so sorry, Lady Felicia," the aged advisor murmured as he led her away. "Such a tragic loss, such a treasonous attack!"

"B-but are we sure she's gone?" the princess sniffed, glancing back. "Can we not..."

"My apologies, sweet lady. None are allowed entry, I tried. Captain Rauksson's orders. But when I spoke to him, he was certain. Please know that nothing, *absolutely nothing* could have been done to save her. We all saw that shot tear clean through her heart."

This only incited a fresh round of tears.

While everyone was thus distracted, Daire slipped through the doors. Quiet reigned within, the silence tomb-like. Appropriate. None were present except Her Majesty – who had been laid carefully on a stone table in the centre of the chamber, directly beneath a shaft of sunlight. Daire's steps echoed across the floor. Up close she was even more stunning. Long manicured nails, hair neatly coiffed, skin like alabaster – save for the smoothly curving stria-lines of indigo which highlighted her exquisite musculature. Her gown was fine yet simple, an elegant amethyst – the colour of royalty. No jewels adorned her person, though. Ataraxia never was one for finery. The years had not changed that. A dribble of red, half-dried, trailed from the corner of her lips, and her delicate cheeks were still flush with pink... her one give-away.

Daire cleared his throat. "You played your part well, Your Grace."

Eyes of the darkest grey fluttered open. So much lay in their depths. Storm clouds and roiling oceans. Mercury and thunder. Hints of blue and green glimmered amid the shadows. Fixing on him, they cleaved like a blade...

Those same eyes that had held his at the garden party when she'd commanded the guard... not to remove the filthy beggar boy from their presence, as he'd expected, but to fetch him some food. "Meat, rice-cakes, and the bread he requested. A bota of water too." What he'd first assumed to be disdain had actually been consideration. Behind her, the Lady Felicia's beatific nose had crinkled with scorn. "Ugh! Don't feed that lice-ridden wretch!" she'd cried. "You don't know where it's *been*." Lady Ataraxia had ignored her sister...

Those same eyes that had looked down imperiously while he'd struggled in the mud of the rain-drenched training yard, once again beaten by his opponent under her keen observation, had held his as she'd reached out... neither to strike nor discipline a failing cadet, as was her right, but, shockingly, to clasp his arm and pull him to his feet, muddying her own hand in the process. Water had run rivulets down her refined cheeks, plastering hair to her skin as in a clear ringing voice, she'd said, "Falling down is good. How else will you learn to get back up again?"

Those same eyes that had held his in the graduation line as she'd bypassed him... only to return with a different medallion. "The Platinum Star suits you best," she'd said, setting it in place. "You've earnt it. I've watched you train for many a year. Seen you return from war battle-scarred and sporting the blood of our enemies. You've practised longer, fought harder, than any other soldier, with a fierceness and valour matched only by our greatest champions." She leaned forward then, her breath a soft brush of air as she whispered into his ear. "Will you become my First Warrior? My Unseen and most honoured Guardsman?"

He'd wanted to say so many things. Chest full, suffused with pride. But when he finally managed to open his mouth, the only words that emerged were, "My life is yours, my lady."

Rauksson, the Captain of the Guards, would have called him a *love-struck young buck*. His training partner would have scoffed "Besotted." But it was more than that. Went deeper. She'd not only earned his love that day but his abject devotion. And with the passing years, through whatever hardships, that had never waned. Only strengthened. He was hers, utterly and completely. Hers to command, her sword to wield. For whatever she deemed necessary.

Those same eyes that he'd grown to adore... held his now.

"That hurt more than expected, Marksman," she said. Toneless, no hint of emotion or pain. Still, he inclined his head. "My apologies, Your Majesty, for the discomfort and for the necessity of the charade. Multiple contractors may have been hired. It had to look authentic."

"Were there others?"

"None that I saw, and my surveillance was very thorough. But we had to be certain."

Her fingers brushed the jagged hole in her bodice. "Your aim was true."

Precise, in fact. Not an inch off.

Daire inclined his head. Praise from her was rare and therefore more worth the earning.

Leaning to the side, she spat a glob of red onto the polished floor – what remained of the blood pellet he'd asked her to use when he'd commed ahead. To make for a convincing show. The spent blood bag came next – retrieved from inside her corset – along with a sheet of discreet metal armour that had allowed for a *non*-lethal strike. Daire knew better than to offer his aid. He did, however, present a handkerchief, which she used to dab at her stained lips as she eased into a sitting position.

"And no others entered here."

"Your standing orders with Captain Rauksson held." He was steadfast, loyal to a fault.

From beneath dark lashes, she regarded him solemnly. "Who was it?" she asked, her voice soft, steady, yet hard as stone. "Who hired you to assassinate me?"

"Your sister, I am sorry to say. With the support of the second and fifth advisors."

It had taken many months and a tedious amount of ferreting to discover these instigators. And their plan.

As soon as Lady Ataraxia had named him First Warrior he'd been dispatched off-world, out into the universe, to seek out any threats to the empire and engage commissions on the imperial heir's lives – which were always plentiful. Years he'd spent cultivating a career as the most sought-after assassin, skilfully dodging the most vulgar calls, to make sure he was the first to know of any new 'work'. Yet for all his efforts, there were some commissions he failed to intercept. This last... had been close. *Too* close for his liking. Because despite Daire's carefully nurtured connections, he'd heard not a whisper of the then-anonymous plotters' search for an actual assassin until that fop in the tavern. Had they approached any other mercenary-for-hire... The call could so easily have gone to another.

Daire took a shaky breath. Best not to think on it. The princess and her accomplices had been unveiled now, their masks ripped away. He still had the holomail – the one with his instructions that he had replayed over and over again during his voyage here – in which a beatific voice, distorted with malice, clearly stated, "*She must die. That throne belongs to Empress Felicia! All hail!*" They may have blitzed the image with static, but the princess's prim timbre was unmistakable. Techs soon confirmed her tonal modulations.

The empress' expression remained blank. But Daire knew her well. Likely no other would have noticed the slight dimming of her brow stria, its blue paling a shade. But he did. He knew to look.

"Felicia has coveted the throne since we were girls. I'd hoped she would be content with the territories I gifted to her but..." She sighed. "While this is a grave disappointment it comes as no surprise."

Ever since her sister had been named heir, Lady Felicia had been unsettled. Even though Ataraxia was the elder. According to one intercepted correspondence, she and her conspirators meant it to be a 'neatly staged bloodless coup'. Because the only casualty was to be the empress. In their calculations, that did not seem to count.

The idea galled, more than Daire would ever let show. He had to suppress the darkening of his striations, keep his temper in check. What made it worse was the crocodilian tears the princess had shed just beyond this chamber's doors. A convincing display too – most would believe that she truly mourned a beloved sister.

"My deepest sympathies, Your Highness." There was nothing else to say.

No sadness. No tears. Not a hint of pain showed despite the enormity of the betrayal. *She's strong.* A fitting ruler. He could have given his life in service to no one less worthy.

"Thank you, Marksman." She inclined her elegant neck. "I am indebted to you."

"As always, I am honoured to serve. What is your next command?"

"Round up the traitors, clap them in irons." Clipped, to the point. And no surprise. Her unrelenting sense of justice was what kept her empire secure.

She rose to her feet, back straight as a pillar of steel. "See it done at once, Marksman."

He bowed. "As you wish, Your Majesty."

One of her pale hands lifted to her temple and the empress's brow furrowed. "Where, pray tell, is my crown?"

"I...believe the last time I saw it, it was in Princess Felicia's hands."

Her facial striations darkened ever so slightly. "I see." Shoulders locked, jaw tense, she turned for the doors. The silk of her amethyst gown whispered over the parquet floor.

"Where are you going, Majesty?"

Half the court was just beyond those doors – grieving subjects who thought her dead.

"To fetch my crown," she said.

Daire could not help the slight smile. His mighty sovereign. What havoc she would wreak on their poor hearts. For the moment they saw her, he knew, she would not so much appear as a ghostly spectre given physical form but as a fiery phoenix risen from the ashes.

Instead of the coronation her sister expected, she attended her own execution. White-faced and shaking. Begging for her life. *Beseeching.* The empress's face was a void, her hands as steady as stone. And as she beheld her sister laid out on the block – quaking, her facial striations blanched to near white – Ataraxia's voice rang out across the courtyard.

"Princess Felicia of House Yii, daughter of the Divine Dynasty, for the crime of high treason against your sovereign, I, Empress Ataraxia the Third, sentence you to die."

"Tara, please!" the young woman sobbed. "I am your *sister*!"

Not a flicker of emotion. "I do only what you meant to have done to me."

The empress nodded to the axeman. He took the few steps to the marble block, raising his laser-edged ceremonial weapon high.

A wail. A downward swing. Swift, lethal. Severing flesh and bone and tendon in one clean, cauterizing blow. It was quick, at least – the one kindness his empress could afford.

Which was more than her traitorous advisors received.

To them, she showed no mercy.

When they began to beg, those who had joined her sister in committing high treason, likely with the sole intent of increasing their own wealth and power, Empress Ataraxia simply held her head high, saying nothing, her eyes like honed steel.

Weakness was for the weak and never could it be said that Ataraxia was thus – rulers who were rarely lasted long. Throughout the screams, Daire stood by her side, strong and unshakable.

There would be no more coup attempts from those unworthy traitors. No more threats to her reign. *Safe again, for now.* With their blood now saturating the ground, something within Daire's chest eased.

"Do you require anything more of me, Your Grace?" he asked, as the executioner sealed the heads in silicon – readying them for display upon the city walls.

Imperious and cool, her face betrayed nothing. Not even her striations rippled. It was but a front – a guise she drew around herself like a shield. He'd learnt that long ago.

"No, Daire. You are dismissed."

It was the first time she had used his name; the first crack in her armour In that moment, as she stared out across her capital city, his heart ached. He wanted nothing more than to step up and wrap her in his arms, to hold her close, to breathe in her storm-cloud scent.

But he could not. Never would.

That was not his role in her life, and his role meant everything.

Instead, he bowed to the waist. "You know how to reach me, Your Majesty. This faithful servant shall always be at your disposal."

Slinking from the last rays of the setting sun, he melted into the encroaching shadows. He would return, whenever she next had need of him. For now, he would track down that old coot who had importuned him in the tavern, who had acted on the traitors' behalf. Not once had Daire's real agenda been suspected, no one knew who his real commander was, and he did not intend for that knowledge to be leaked now.

Nemma Wollenfang is a prize-winning speculative fiction writer who lives in Northern England. Her work has appeared in several venues, including: *Abyss & Apex, Speculatively Queer, Broken Eye Books,* and Flame Tree Publishing for their *Gothic Fantasy* series. She is a recipient of the Speculative Literature Foundation's Working Class Writers Grant and a participant of Writers on the Moon. She can be found on Facebook and Amazon.

Galleons

by Allen Ashley

We were galleons but we didn't know it. Too swift to relish and absorb our moment of pomp and finery in the sea-sparkling sun. Just tall, proud, vital vessels, creating the currents, ushering in a new wave that ultimately might be seen to not differ too much from earlier iterations. You watched us glide swan-like as we cleaved the waters. Majestic, unsinkable.

We were pirates and we might have had an inkling: stealing references from old songs and films and TV programmes and those books we never wanted to study in sixth form or college yet were imprinted on us still. We didn't recognise our actions were futile, anachronistic – we believed we could still find that buried treasure, one day soon.

We are ghost ships. Hardly even fit for salvage. Who cares where we go or what ripples we create? No-one fixes a telescope or a periscope upon our passing. You might stumble upon records of us in old charts and logs or even be amazed that we are still sailing *somewhere* today... but off the main drag and never glinting in the sunlight. One voyage away from a shipwreck or a wrecking crew.

Allen Ashley is the founder of the advanced science fiction and fantasy group Clockhouse London Writers. Allen has a new chapbook coming out from Eibonvale Press in 2023. Entitled *Journey to the Centre of the Onion*, it is the most Allen Ashley story in many a year and is not to be missed. Aside from that, during March 2023, Allen will be guest editing the online magazine *Sein und Werden*. Amongst his recent publications are pieces in *The World of Myth* and the NAWE magazine *Writing in Education*.

And I Will Make Thy Name Great

by Louis Evans

Abraham, the potter's son, was sweeping out the workshop late one night, the air hot, the sweat beading on his brow, the kiln still radiating the baking heat it had absorbed over the course of the day.

This was when he heard the voice.

"Boy!"

Abraham looked around.

No source of the voice was apparent. No person had stepped into the shed, nor were the flames of a djinn visible. Four copies of the idol of Suen, god of the moon and chief among gods, were cooling on the shelf opposite the kiln, and sometimes Suen spoke to believers, but the idols were not yet consecrated and certainly could not host the presence of the god. No raven perched in the workshop's eaves, croaking out an imitation of speech. Abraham was baffled.

"Boy! You, boy!"

Abraham spun around and pointed to his chest with an exaggerated flourish.

"Me?" he asked the empty room.

"Yes, you! Abraham, son of Terah!"

"Who are you?"

"I am the Lord your G-d, creator of the universe, ruler of heaven and earth, and my name is—"

And it seemed to Abraham that the voice at this time spoke a name, a name of majesty and awe, but Abraham did not speak that name again for all of his days.

Abraham was no priest or initiate but he knew how to conduct himself

63

in the presence of a god and so he prostrated himself on the floor, grateful that he had nearly finished sweeping when the Lord spoke to him, so that he would not get his face dirty.

"Yes, Lord?" asked Abraham, son of Terah the potter, of the city of Haran.

And the unnamable Lord spoke to Abraham, saying,

Go from thy country, thy people and thy father's home
to the land I will show thee.
I will make of thee a great nation,
and I will bless thee.
Thou wilt be a blessing, and
I will make thy name great.

Abraham remained prostrate on the floor, and he gave thanks that he was Abraham, son of Terah the potter, and that his father had taught him that the small tradesman is his own man, equal among all the lords of all the Earth, and that greatness may inspire respect but it cannot compel obeisance. And Abraham the potter's son spake to the Lord, saying, "No, thank you."

Silence.

Abraham considered lifting his head just ever so slightly to see what was happening, but ultimately decided against it.

When the voice came again, it seemed slightly less confident.

"Pardon?"

"No, thank you," said Abraham to the Lord his G-d, creator of the Universe, ruler of Heaven and Earth, and then he added "my Lord," just in case it was necessary.

And once more the Lord spoke to Abraham, saying, "Are you sure you understood me just then?"

Abraham nodded. "Yes, O Lord. I understood your offer. You are most gracious, but no thank you."

And the Lord spoke unto Abraham, saying, "But I really think perhaps you didn't understand me just then."

And the Lord gave unto Abraham a vision of his life as Patriarch. A vision of wives and servants; of many large tents and retainers; of caravans of camels and troops of sons and grandsons, following him through the desert from oasis to oasis; of descendants as numerous as the stars. And the Lord caused to pass before Abraham the likenesses of countless men and women who reached out to him, calling him father, patriarch, progenitor, and Abraham heard his name spoken by men and women from the ages to come, blessing each other in his name and passing on his birthright, and truly these generations were as numberless as the stars in the sky.

And it was a mighty vision, and Abraham was sorely tempted.

But then he thought of Sarai, his betrothed, and the life they meant to live in Haran, and the family of reasonable size that they would raise in his father's household. And he thought of his inheritance, a small business of good reputation in the local community, which he would squander if, like his father, he moved from city to city.

And, also, Abraham had a sneaking suspicion that if the Lord had wanted him to go anywhere particularly pleasant or even reasonably convenient, the Lord probably would have referred to that specific place by name, rather than pussyfooting around it with all of that "to a land that I will show you" nonsense.

And so Abraham, still prostrate on the floor, said unto the Lord for a third time, "No thank you."

"Well," said the Lord his G-d, Creator of the Universe, Ruler of Heaven and Earth, whose name may not be spoken. "If it's going to be like that, then fine."

And the presence of the Lord departed, and Abraham the potter's son was alone in the workshop, and he stood up and finished the sweeping.

And Abraham married Sarai and had a regular number of children, regardless of what anyone had thought about her infertility, and inherited his father's business, and lived as a potter in the city of Haran for all of his days.

And his children had children, and those children had children, and soon enough none knew that they were descended from Abraham son of Terah. And they spread out in the way that descendants do, moving for jobs or spouses and that sort of thing, but not, to choose an example completely at random, moving to a foreign dynasty and being enslaved for centuries and following a pillar of fire through a desert or anything noteworthy like that.

And so it was years later that one of those descendants was David, the shepherd boy, living in the hills of Canaan.

Saul was king in Canaan in those days, and the Philistines made war upon Canaan, and in the Valley of Elah the two armies were encamped. And the Philistines sent forth the giant Goliath, who challenged the Canaanites to single combat, but none would face him.

Meanwhile David was up in the hills, tending to the sheep, which meant, you know, hanging out on a hill. Nailing the occasional wolf with his slingshot. Shepherd stuff.

And the Lord spake to David, saying, "Shepherd boy!" And after some low comedy around introductions and mysterious voices and whatnot, the Lord made his pitch, and He spake to David, saying,

Go from thy hillside, down into the valley
and smite the Philistine with your sling stone.
I will make of thee a great king,
and I will bless thy nation.
Thou wilt be a blessing, and
I will make thy name great.

"Let me get this straight," said David.

"Take your time," said the Lord, whose words were more patient than His tone of voice.

"You want me, a full-time shepherd, part-time harpist, to go down into the valley."

"Yes."

"Where the armies are fighting."

"Yes."

"And you want me to go kill a giant with, basically, a pebble."

"That's right."

"And in exchange for this suicide mission you are offering . . . pretty much just fame?"

And the Lord could tell which way this conversation was going, and so He made to pass before David a vision of the life of a king. A vision of battle and glory, of the conquest of Jerusalem, city of milk and honey, fortress of the Jebusites. A vision of countless wives and countless concubines; of rich tributes, a palace of cedar, chests of gold and treasures of jewels; of a great temple of the Lord erected in gleaming marble; of steles bearing his name and the name of his house; of conquests in his name; of proud sons of noble bearing; of a dynasty for the ages.

And David was a young boy, thrilled by glory and adventure, and sorely tempted. But he remembered the sheep, and the quiet days he had spent on the hillside, and he spoke to the Lord, saying, "Nah."

For unlike a potter's son, who must learn to talk to customers, a shepherd boy talks mostly to his sheep and can easily grow up into a real asshole.

"Ugh," said the Lord his G-d, Creator of the Universe, Ruler of Heaven and Earth, and He left.

And David stayed on the hill with his sheep, and the armies of the Philistines and the Canaanites came to a diplomatic agreement that nobody really liked, but at least it avoided open bloodshed. And Goliath did not die in battle, yet still he died shortly thereafter, of congestive heart failure. For the years are not kind to a man who is six cubits tall.

And in the years that followed the land was conquered repeatedly, by the Assyrians, Babylonians, Achaemenids, Hellenes, Seleucids, and at last the Romans from across the sea, for everyone wants a piece of the land called Palestine. Truly it is God's own country.

But *only* in the sense that it is a beautiful land and pleasant to reside there. Not in any sort of larger, theopolitical kind of way.

In those days Herod was king in Palestine, because you can't keep a bad guy down, even if you wind up as hard as you can and dickpunch the prime timeline right in the Patriarchs. And in those days was born Yeshua, son of Joseph, who grew up to become a carpenter.

One warm afternoon Yeshua was in his workshop, planing a plank of wood, and the Lord came to Yeshua, saying, "Yeshua, son of Joseph!"

"Yes?" said Yeshua, and he continued planing the timber with iron and rule, because he was a pretty laid back guy and so skipped past the whole "a mysterious voice is addressing me by name, how alarming" stage of things.

And the Lord, heartened by this attitude, spake unto Yeshua of Bethlehem, son of Joseph, saying,

> Go up to Jerusalem, home of King Herod
> Preach there a new and godly faith
> I will make of thee a great prophet,
> and I will bless thy teachings.
> Thou wilt be a blessing, and
> I will make thy name great.

And Yeshua continued planing for a few more strokes, until the Lord despaired of his ever replying. Whereupon Yeshua spoke unto the Lord his G-d, and he said,

"No, I don't think it's for me."

"What?"

"Prophecy, religious leadership. It's harder than it sounds to set people on the right path. Out of the crooked timber of humanity, no straight thing was ever made."

"Oh, that's clever. You make that one up yourself?"

Yeshua was not listening to the sarcasm of the Lord. Instead he was rubbing his hand contemplatively on his beard.

"But out of the timber of, you know, regular timber, I've made some pretty great chairs."

"Chairs."

"Tables, too."

"I offer you the greatest role in all of human history, founder of the world's most populous religion, and you're going to pass on that because you prefer . . . chairs."

"Have you ever made a really good chair, O Lord?"

"I am the Lord your God, ruler of the universe, maker of all things visible and invisible!"

Yeshua finished planing the wood. He brushed away the shavings with a rag and took out a chisel, and began to notch the plank by hand.

"Nevertheless," said the Lord, "I admit I haven't done much with chairs. Personally. As such."

"You give a man the first good chair of his life and watch him sit down in it, and you'll see a face with more bliss than you thought possible. When people hear preaching, they mostly just end up feeling guilty."

And the Lord felt that He had well and truly lost control of the discussion at this point, and so He caused to pass before Yeshua a vision of his ministry: of faithful disciples hanging on his every word; of throngs of seekers kneeling at his feet; of miracles of the raising of the dead and the multiplication of loaves and fishes; of turning out the great temple of Zeus in Jerusalem and the moneychangers there; of a new Church named after his teaching; of missionaries, monks, bishops, popes, priests, nuns; of songs and sculpture and masterpieces; of men and women speaking in a thousand tongues always to praise his name and to give each other solace.

And Yeshua saw that there was much good he could do, yet he suspected that much evil might come of it as well. And he saw the crosses that the faithful would wear, and he thought of the field in Golgotha where the Roman legions executed condemned criminals by means of crucifixion, and he thought, when you got down to it in the end, a cross was a pretty unwholesome use of wood.

Compared to a chair.

And Yeshua opened his eyes from the vision and the Lord his God saw his expression and was like, "Don't even bother to tell me, I get it," and so the Lord disappeared.

And Yeshua, son of Joseph, lived to a ripe old age, and married a nice Jewish girl named Mary — as well over fifty percent of women in the area were named at the time — and had children, and made a series of very well regarded chairs, so that wealthy Roman citizens said if you needed some furniture in Palestine you could do no better than going to Bethlehem.

And the years turned.

And faiths rose and fell. And the Emperor converted to Mithraism and the next Emperor converted to Platonism and a third Emperor married a horse, and the barbarians rose in the West and the Persians and Arabs rose in the East and the Empire fell, not all at once but bit by bit, like a tablecloth being yanked off the edge of the table by a cat over the course of centuries.

And one day in Aachen, the city whose name sounds like a sneeze, there was a young boy named Charles, the mayor's son, sitting out in the garden.

And the Lord came to Charles and said,

> Claim thou the kingdom thy father will leave you
> Take up thy sword and thy father's throne
> I will make of thee a great king,
> and I will bless thy nation.
> Thou wilt be a legend, and
> I will make thy name great.

But Charles knew what his father Pepin had done to young Childeric, first making him king of the Franks with many expansive promises, and then later having Childeric decapitated and claiming the throne for himself. And so Charles had learned the lesson that only the wise learn, which is to look every gift horse in the mouth, with advanced dental tools if necessary.

And so Charles spoke to the Lord, saying, "What precisely must I do?"

And the Lord replied to Charles with the voice of one who is waving a hand about idly, as if to say, "Oh, it's nothing", and he spake to Charles, saying,

"Just poison your brother, assume the throne, conquer Saxony, Bavaria, the Kingdom of the Lombards, bits of Spain, that sort of thing."

"And what will you give me?"

"I will increase your lands and your fiefdoms, and I will cause you to be acclaimed Emperor, in the temples of, ugh, *Odin* and *Jupiter*—" When the Lord spoke the name of these gods, he did so with resentful disdain, and there followed, at this time, the unmistakable sound of an unseen mouth violently grinding invisible teeth.

"—and I will make your name so great that everyone will stick the word "great" right onto the end of your name and leave it there!"

And in that time and that place, where all the barbarians spoke Latin and the Romans spoke mostly Greek, the offer meant that Charles would always be known as Carolus Magnus, or Charlamagne.

And the boy who could be Charlamagne thought about this offer, and the Lord did not need to make a vision pass before him, because it did so all on its own. A vision of armies, of serried ranks of cavalry, of castles besieged, of an

Imperial coronation in the temple of Jupiter in Rome, of tapestries to his glory and manuscripts recounting his deeds, of endless tributes from the Slavs and envoys from the Saracens. And all this seemed pretty great to Charles.

But then he thought about how his father was never home, always off conquering this or subduing that, and how the crown of the Franks weighed upon him as the yoke upon the oxen, and Charles the First shook his head at the Lord, and said, "No thank you, I think I'll focus on internal improvements and legal reform."

And the Lord left, though he could be heard to mutter "Are you kidding Me?" as he did so.

And Charles the First ascended to his father's throne and was promptly poisoned by his brother Carloman instead of the other way around.

And the Frankish kingdom grew and it shrank, and the Spanish and Lombard kingdoms grew and they shrank, and Kings and peoples did an elaborate stochastic dance for centuries, and the Mongols arrived and then left for some reason, and there were never any Crusades, as the kings of the West saw no particular reason to invade a bit of the eastern Mediterranean which had been captured by the Turks, and all the kingdoms bore the names of duchies or principalities you have never heard of. And boats got better and some asshole "discovered" the "New World", which is really just the leftmost bit of the same old world if you think about it, and the kings of the West were pretty terrible about the whole thing, with colonies and smallpox and so forth, and the lands of the New World became their own nations, like Vespuccia and Montreal and Texas.

And in the isle of Brittania in the North Sea, where they worship the god with horns of a stag, one man invented the machine loom and another one invented the steam engine, and all of a sudden the Industrial Revolution was on like Donkey Kong.

And the peasants left the farms and came to the cities and worked in factories for pittances, and in place of lords and serfs there were capitalists and laborers, and the workers' lives were bitter with harsh labor with steel and concrete and all sorts of work in machinery, and in all their harsh labor the bosses worked them ruthlessly.

And in this age was born Karl, son of Heinrich Marx the lawyer, of the line of Abraham and David, though obviously nobody had ever heard of Abraham or David, and he grew up in Trier in Prussia.

And Karl went to college in Bonn, where he wished to study philosophy and his father wished him to study law and they exchanged angry letters about it often, by the excellent Prussian postal service, because in every Prussia in every timeline the mail always comes on time.

And one night while Karl was composing an especially impassioned letter to his father, the Lord came to Karl Marx and He spake, saying,

> Go down to Berlin, crown jewel of Prussia
> Join thou the Communist Party there,
> I will make of thee a great writer,
> and I will bless thy Party.
> Thou wilt found an empire, and
> I will make thy name great.

And Karl, who had been raised by rationalists and by liberal humanists, spoke, saying, "Am I hallucinating?"

And the Lord spake to Karl and said, "Listen, kid, you're not my first choice either but we can at least be civil about it. I Am That I Am, the Lord thy G-d, unnamed and unnamable."

And Karl said, "I am pretty sure that gods don't exist, and that religion is the opiate of the masses, and that Allfather Odin is just a myth."

And the Lord said, "Got it in one, Karl, but I am the real deal."

And Karl said, "But if you exist, Lord, then why not Odin? Or Athena? Or Karya, the supreme god of the Turks? Or—"

And the Lord said, "Listen, we're getting a little off topic, here, let's just skip straight to the vision. Yes? Good?"

And before Karl could reply, the Lord caused to pass before his eyes a vision of the future, driven by the iron laws of dialectical materialism; of the springtime revolutions in Berlin and Paris and Kyiv and Volgograd; of years of underground preaching and secret meetings and pamphlets; of general strikes and mass uprisings, of the fall of the Tartar Czar and the Chinese Emperor; of the dictatorship of the proletariat; of the industrialization of the great Eurasian hinterland; of rebels in Latin America and Africa and Indochina; and of countless men and women of all races and all stations, arguing with one another, brandishing books to one another, and on each cover of the book his name; of great Premiers and Potentates standing before the world on electrotelemagnetic screens and proclaiming the gospel of Marxism to the planet.

And Karl was a freshman in college, so he was not exactly surprised to see himself become a figure of world-historical import but still it felt pretty nice.

But he thought about those revolutions, and the years spent in hiding, being dragged off and tortured by secret police, and the years spent in power, having other people dragged off and tortured by secret police, and it felt a little, you know, time is a flat circle, and not at all like the glorious future of equality of which he had dreamed.

So Karl said "No, thank you" to the Lord, who disappeared in a sigh of disappointment but also relief, for, frankly, He had had pretty mixed feelings from the jump about getting involved with organized atheism.

And Karl got his law degree, and did some pro bono work for labor organizations, but never really got involved in radical journalism. And there were workers revolts and peasant revolts and nationalist revolts and they all had their own philosophies and names. And the nineteenth century begat the twentieth century, and there was a war to end all wars, and then another war after that, and plenty of genocides, though none of the Jews, who had never existed in the first place, and the radio sang and the atom split and the great powers glared at each other and divvied up the globe and then the globe decided to undivvy itself, which was pretty awkward, and then came some moon landings and a computer printed HELLO, WORLD!, and there was Jimi Hendrix.

And in the fullness of time the Lord came to me, across the ocean and across a continent from Prussia, in the city of Yerba Buena, in the state of Alta California, in the Republic of Greater Texas, and he spake unto me, saying, "Hey kid, wanna be huge on Twitter?"

"Not really," I said.

And the Lord made to pass before my eyes a vision of likes and retweets and a verified checkmark; and of the social media thinkfluencers who would follow me. And I spake to the Lord, saying, "Honestly that whole lifestyle seems like a hot mess, thanks anyway."

And the Lord sighed, saying, "Yeah, alright," and made as if to depart.

And I spoke unto the Lord, saying "Hey, buddy, you seem beat. Come, stay with me. Eat of my pizza. Tell me all about it."

And the Lord told unto me the story I have just now related, from the patriarch without a patrimony to the abdicated atheist, to my own day.

And I thought, you know, maybe this has to do with *His* issues? An unnamed G-d obsessed with making someone else's name great?

But I didn't bring it up, because it seemed like the Lord was having a hard day.

"Hey, O Lord," said I, "wanna hang out for a bit and watch the Great Brittania Bake-off on Netflix?"

And the Lord G-d, Ruler of the Universe, Creator of Heaven and Earth, spake, saying, "Yeah, I'd like that a lot."

And so we did. And no names were made great, but pastries certainly were.

Louis Evans met the love of his life on the street and now they're married with two cats. Meet cute, happy ending. It's good work, if you can find it. His writing has appeared in *Vice, The Magazine of Fantasy & Science Fiction, Nature: Futures, Analog SF&F, Interzone* and more. He's online at evanslouis.com and on Mastodon at @louisevans @wandering.shop

Ring

by Sadie Maskery

Triumphant, stupid as a fox
drunk on blood in the henhouse,
you refused the flame
to grab the eternal prize.
Predictable. And now
we tell our children,
trembling in their beds,
how it perverted you.
That is your doom,
no grand fall, just reduction
to a fairytale. Silly ghoul,
bogeyman of grief and hate,
mouth stretched by howls,
flesh rubbed and worn
like onionskin beneath the black...
your whole being has dwindled
to inkblots from a dreamer's pen.
You cannot kill a dead soul
though you tried, how you tried
those nights when infinity
screamed back at you
and we turned the page.

Sadie Maskery lives in Scotland by the sea. Her first chapbook, *Push*, is published by Erbacce Press and her full collection, *Shouting at Crows*, by Alien Buddha Press. Her second chapbook is in production for late 2023. She can be found on Twitter as @saccharinequeen.

Portrait Of A Flower

by R. Leigh Hennig

A t night, a sound.

Shelly raises her head. Marin says don't worry, that things are fine. This is a lie.

She turns over, away, and pulls a pillow over her head to dull the sounds of the city and the street from two stories below.

Soft snores, unaware. He envies her this. For a moment he allows his mind an indulgence in fantasy, permits himself, in the softening hours of the early morning, to again consider the options before him, to imagine there existed any alternative for what he knows he must do.

He could call the police. Used to be a time when they took care of things like this, when theirs was an institution not completely broken and lacking in purpose or morality. If he could just talk to them, provide the evidence he found when the addict he calls his brother left his phone in their apartment—

No. He tried that once already. It doesn't matter that he has proof that his brother plans on breaking into their apartment, that he's done it so many times before. They weren't interested then, they aren't interested now, and he doesn't have enough for another bribe. "*Protection fee*," he mutters into the dark, his face a mask of bitterness and contempt. The thought turns his stomach and so he dismisses it; he doesn't like the way it makes him feel.

Social services, then? How many times has he called, stopped by their local office, practically on his knees? They were clear there would be no shortcutting the waitlist, measured in years, and anyway Cormac would have to agree to treatment. Another dead end.

There are no friends. No family. They won't speak to him anymore, won't have anything more to do with Cormac. Those bridges have been burnt too many times.

The hospitals, such as they are, are little more than funnels for the morgues. He remembers a song from his youth, about checking into a hotel but being unable to check out.

No, he thinks, again with contempt. Those are not places for healing. Maybe they would give him Panadol , and what good is that?

Cormac cannot be made sober. He doesn't want to be. Marin knows this, knows deep down, knows it the way he knows he and Shelly can never have children but continue to try anyway because *what if?*

The addiction is not his brother's fault. This is a thing he tells himself over and over and over again, a broadcast on repeat, dull, incessant, a painful throbbing that has been there and will always be there and is yet unhelpful, still. It reminds him of a fable about a scorpion and a frog. But he wonders: is Cormac the scorpion, or is he the frog?

Maybe both, he thinks. *Maybe I'm the frog. Maybe I'm the scorpion.*

Another sound from the kitchen below, the trash can turned over. He stares at the ceiling and the neon light that comes through the yellowed shades from the flickering billboard across the street. *Live girls*, it reads, the dim and broken "*L*" a reflection of what is within. Rain falls against the window like tears, soft and long.

He sits up in bed, rubs the deep hollows of his eyes. He checks his phone — 2:17 — and sets it too close to the edge.

A sharp clatter. It falls to the cold tile, the sound of it naked and stark in the stillness, almost accusatory as if an alarm to the betrayal he will soon commit.

Shelly stirs. He freezes, holds his breath. He doesn't want her awake for this, for what's to come. She's suffered enough already.

After a moment, her snoring resumes. He lets out a breath before rising, bending to retrieve the phone with its screen now cracked.

He uses the light from his phone to find the syringe he'd been hiding in their closet. His instinct is to recoil from the touch of it, as if bitten, before removing the plastic cap over the needle and shining the phone's light against its transparent body.

The dosage is there, just like it was the last time he checked. 0.5ml. Barely anything at all. *Is this really all it takes?* he recalls asking the man he'd met in the stairwell of the old parking garage. The man had said nothing after taking his money, turning instead to leave him alone with his many questions. It would have to be. It was all he could afford.

Marin walks slowly across the hall and down the stairs to the sounds coming from his kitchen, carrying himself like someone with the familiarity of age, despite his youth.

Light switch on the wall. It would be better to do this in the dark — easier, maybe — but no. He will not be that coward that will not look his brother in the face. The light comes on and slowly, slowly, the addict before him turns.

"Hey, Cormac," he says, trying on a wan smile. It doesn't fit. "Come and sit with me. Let's talk."

His eyes are shiny, bits of steely flint that catch and hold the light peculiarly. It's the excessive moisture in them that does that, another side effect from the drug that's destroyed his life. His movements are slow, glacial, and not for the first time he wonders if his brother is aware of what's become of him. Does he think normally when high? Is it just his movement that is impaired? Or are his thoughts — reduced as they are by the drug they call *slow* — also impaired?

He ignores the biting stink of Cormac's unwashed body and takes him by the arm, leading him gently to the couch in the living room. He reeks of ammonia because he's pissed himself, garbage because that's where he's been digging, and rot because that's what he's been eating.

Together they sit, Cormac an unwitting participant, his sloth-like movements little able to resist. He's not sure if he'll be able to understand him in his current state, but he decides to try anyway, to make his peace with the older man, because, after the injection, he knows there will be little left at all. That there is much of anything since the addiction took hold is something that Marin knows, but like the knowledge that the addiction is not Cormac's fault, it is a thing he knows, different and not at all the same as what he *knows*

"Do you remember the speech you gave at our wedding?" A smile. "I doubt it. You were pretty drunk. So was I. I don't remember what you said, but I remember how you made me feel: welcome. Safe. Loved, like I belonged.

wish we could both feel that way again. I wish Tab could feel that way. It's hard for her, you know? Our sister doesn't see what you've become. She still sees who you once were. She can't get it out of her head, that image of you as a boy. I think that's why it hurts her so much."

His hands begin to shake. His throat is growing tight, tears forming in his eyes. Quickly, before he can lose his nerve, he reaches over and stabs the needle into the meat of his brother's thigh. No chance to think this through anymore, to convince himself there's another way. He knows there's not. *Knows* it.

Nothing happens. He begins to doubt the dosage of the so-called 'cure,' to curse his stupidity for meeting the man in the stairwell of the abandoned parking garage and spending what little they didn't have to spare. But then Cormac gasps, sucking in air as if he'd been drowning. He stiffens, the muscles in his body constricting. The violent reaction is not unexpected; he had read that this would happen. Still, it is a surprise to watch it happen in person, to see how the body responds as one drug counteracts another. He braces himself for what he knows will happen next: seconds that will last for Marin an eternity, the last time he will ever speak to his older brother — his *real* brother — again.

"Marin? What's happening? Where am I?" Gritted teeth, clenched jaw, Cormac's speech is strained, his voice hoarse. It's a moment of lucidity as the addiction is broken and he is instantly sobered before the cure completes the rewiring of the neurons in his brain. It throws out the addiction, but it also throws out so much more.

"You're home," Marin says. "You're safe now. I'm going to take care of you."

"Wait, wait. Just wait a minute, okay? Stop. Y-y-y-you promised. P-promised. I can stop. I can go to rehab. I can b-b-be better," Cormac says, his body beginning to convulse. Foam bubbles out of one corner of his mouth. Understanding. He knows what he's been given, knows what it will do to him, his dreams, his potential. Still, he tries to reason with the inevitable. "S-s-stop, I can, can, c-c-caaahhhuuuuggggh."

Marin forces himself to watch the light in his brother's eyes die, become glazed, take a look that will stay that way until he dies many years later.

Muscles relax. Cormac sits up, jaw slack. He grunts, the only way he will ever again be able to communicate. But the addiction is finally broken. A demon exorcised, like from a movie.

Marin stands, takes Cormac by the hand. In the bathroom, clean clothes have already been set out. Marin undresses his brother, turns on the shower water. On the wall is a portrait of a flower, colourful hues of red and orange. Cormac sees it, and begins to smile. He grunts, reaches for the flower that is not.

"That's right, Cormac. That's a flower. You painted that for me two years ago, remember? For my birthday."

Grubby fingers, nails broken and impacted with grime, grope at the picture frame.

"Come on," Marin says, guiding what remains of the other man to the shower. "Let's get you cleaned up."

R. Leigh Hennig writes mostly horror from New England, with stories having appeared in anthologies by Crystal Lake Publishing, Weird Little Worlds, Flame Tree Press, and the HWA Poetry Showcase vol. IX. He keeps an irregularly updated blog at https://semioticstandard.com but is most active on Mastodon https://wandering.shop/@semioticstandard

A Jar Full Of R's
by Sally Gander

When Alexandra heard an argument break out on the street below her living room window, she knew it was time to go out to gather mentations. She'd been putting it off, but the jars were nearly empty and she had a new client the following day.

She pulled on her boots and jacket, and once outside she found the argument was still going on, a man shouting, "We're all here because we work, but you wander around all day taking up energy, expecting *us* to move out of the way for *you*?"

The pavement was clogged with tired workers waiting at the tram stop; the shouting man, dressed in a shabby suit, was spitting rage at an elderly woman who wanted to make her way through the crowd, most of whom were absorbed in their tablets or listening to music on their headphones.

"Don't be an idiot," Alexandra said to him. "Just let her pass."

The man barely flinched, just aimed a "Fuck you" at her and turned to the road as the clattering tram arrived.

She'd learned to be careful in the way she engaged with these confrontations. She wanted his words and his rage, but she didn't want to illicit any more than that, and she didn't want to engage with the elderly woman who was trying to thank her. Alexandra had no use for kindness. If people were more kind, there would be no need for her trade at all, and anyway, all that niceness reduced the quantity of mentations she was able to gather. Much better to harvest the anger, wash it and turn it into something useful. She liked the symmetry of this. The cure extracted from the problem, like penicillin extracted from mould.

The crowd filtered its way onto the tram and the elderly woman made her way forward, Alexandra turning to walk in the opposite direction. She imagined the woman's own rage, how left behind by the world she felt, how her children had abandoned her, how she'd worked hard her whole life and for what? Misery and poverty and ignorance, and young people who think they can shout at her to release their own tensions.

She let these thoughts run around in her head as she walked the littered streets, seeking out the poorest slums and squats, the vandalised shops and abandoned churches, the places where despair manifested itself in bitter resentment. She was particularly watchful today. For a few weeks now she had the feeling that she was being watched, perhaps even followed. She wondered if her past was finally catching up with her, or perhaps it was the street police.

Her trade was illegal so she couldn't be too careful, but she'd done everything she could to keep under the radar. The shop below her flat wasn't obviously a shop, with an entrance that could only be accessed by the gated alleyway along the side of the building. She rarely took new clients, and when she did it was always through a recommendation from an existing, trusted client.

Then there were the drug gangs. She had an uneasy agreement with the local crew to keep out of each other's way, but all it took was a shift in power or a drop in their profits and she'd be fucked. When there was a drug that could sort out your head instead of destroying it, tolerance and diplomacy became an elusive commodity.

She hoped it wasn't a customer who'd had a bad reaction to their blend. Back when she did her training with Adjei, he told her stories of psychosis and schizophrenia if the words weren't cleansed properly. But the scare stories seemed like urban myths to her, maybe propaganda put out by the government, who wanted to keep people dosed with narcotic powders and cheap alcohol, keep them poor and dependent so the politicians were free to enforce their laws.

She let these thoughts spiral as she walked past the medical centre, the queue longer today. Desperate people stood lost inside their need; a little girl who had a rash of hives across her face looked up at Alexandra with red-crusted eyes. There weren't enough doctors or therapists to make a dent in

A Jar Full Of R's

the prison of poverty this side of the river had become, and here was where she felt the necessity of her trade more than anywhere. She wished she could hand out cards so they could find her, so they could know there was some kind of hope, but the risks were too high and she'd still have to charge, she had to earn a living somehow.

She came to the tenement blocks where her paranoia became justified. A gang of young men was getting high in the shadows of the graffitied walkways and shouted at her with lustful threats. She felt unsafe and vulnerable, picking her way through dumped fridges and rusting bicycles without so much as a knife for protection. But it was rich material for gathering, so she let the aggression of their words pummel into her own reactive defences, creating a soup of mentatious thought that drove her on.

She walked through the sprawling park where the homeless slept beneath the trees, a spread of grubby mattresses and torn cardboard, many of them huddled beneath layers of blankets. One woman was sitting up and rocking, tattoos snaking their way up her neck and curling over her chin. She was muttering what seemed to be a series of angry questions, but her eyes were glazed and lost in whatever she'd sniffed or swallowed or injected, a mottled dog beside her baring his teeth and growling. Alexandra absorbed her words and responded with her own raging questions. Why didn't she get a job? Couldn't she at least wash at the public toilets, for fuck's sake?

And finally she reached the edge of the park, a place she dreaded yet couldn't help but return to. There was a playpark here: the swings were just hanging chains and a roundabout had been tipped onto its side, the rusted climbing frame the only game that remained playable. There were a few boys here today, but Alexandra couldn't bear to look at their hollow cheeks and the hungry look in their eyes.

She walked past them and climbed onto the wall, sitting on the top with her legs dangling as though she was out for a picnic, looking down at the thick snaking river and the suspension bridge with its checkpoint and armoured patrols.

The first time she found this spot, just a few weeks before meeting Adjei, her vision was jittery with the brown powder she'd swallowed and she'd gazed at the financial district beyond the river, the place where her father had

83

made his money. She felt the shame of that money, and the responsibility of enjoying the spoils of her father's deceit. She and her mother had lived surrounded by beauty and comfort; her mother was a gently guiding spirit oblivious of the true nature of the man she'd married. They had everything they could ever want, but they had an abundance of ignorance too, and in her high state she'd laughed a snorting, manic shriek, buzzed that it was all gone, her father in prison, her mother dead. In that moment, her stomach had cramped with hunger and she wished she'd done the same as her mother, let herself drop into the river to become a black bloated corpse.

She wondered what would have happened if she hadn't met Adjei. If he hadn't pulled her out of her self-destruction to give her a trade, something that contributed instead of destroying. She felt a sob well up inside her, the despair that always dug deep when she was out gathering, her mind infected with sorrow and all the bad things that happened in the world.

She reminded herself of Adjei's mantra... *gather so that you can give...* and jumped down from the wall to head back to the flat the quick route through the shopping precinct. When she passed the tattoo parlour she raised a hand to Max, who was chatting to a client in the doorway. She'd spent many hours on his couch, the last a full sleeve on her right arm – abstract shapes intersected with thick black lines. At the time she'd thought the bold reds and greens that filled the shapes were an emblem of her escape, but when she looked at her arm now all she saw was grey lines, faded colours and loneliness, much the same as when she looked in a mirror.

She lowered her head and continued walking, the gathered mentations thick and heavy and swirling in loops of rage, her feet aching, her forehead pulsing with tension. She only saw the dark tarmac and her boots, only heard the thud thud thud of her steps, sensing that she was alone in her isolation and that no-one was watching or following today.

In her living room, she kicked her boots off and didn't bother switching on the lamp, even though night was closing in and the shadows made her worry about the intruders and rapists who stalked the city on the lookout for women like her who lived alone. She sat at the table in front of the Wernicke machine. Adjei made it for her when she was ready to go out on her own, repurposing an old portable TV set and building a printer into its base. He took out the inner workings and lined the inside with waterproofing polymer to hold the cleansing solution, fixed a housing to the top to hold a double ink cartridge, and on top of that, the microprocessor. She'd seen other machines made of microwave ovens, radios and even a fish tank, anything that could be found on the street or bought cheap at an exchange store. The switches on the front had been rewired and finely calibrated, but they still had their TV labelling so if she got raided it could pass muster as the genuine article. If they were in a hurry, that was. If they weren't, they'd see the paper slotted into the printer in the base. They'd see the sticky pads at the end of long wires attached to the microprocessor. They'd see the only program this TV would ever show was cleansing solution and ink and a fuck load of bad thoughts getting washed.

She picked up the pads and pressed them to the left side of her head, one to the Wernicke, the other to the Broca. She wanted the words out of her brain now, wanted to be rid of them. She flicked on the switch and the stand-by light flashed red, then settled to a consistent green that illuminated the room in a comforting way. She turned the configuration button and repeated her name in her head, *Alexandra West, Alexandra West,* the pads buzzing against her temple and the cartridge releasing its ink into the solution. The clear liquid turned a hazy grey which drifted and began to formulate shapes, blurred and indistinct, rough assimilations of an A, an n, a couple of x's, like soft wisps of river weed caught on the current. They became more solid and clear as they drifted to the bottom, and below, the printer started whirring and clunking and pushed out a piece of damp paper with her name running along the top.

She put it to one side and pressed the reset button, sat back and closed her eyes, letting the harvest of her thoughts run and run, all the vile things she'd heard and seen, the rage she felt when she listened to the news on the radio earlier in the day, the wars, the famine, the murders and child abductions. The anger acted like a relentless engine, the Wernicke machine pumping a steady stream of ink to keep up, the solution bubbling and turning behind the screen, letters drifting and stabilising, drifting and stabilising until they were washed of the dirty hate from the street, and the printer started up again so the words could spill out with their new, pure clarity. Words... letters... symbols... punctuation. On and on it went, her mind emptying into the machine, the solution cleansing the words onto the paper.

She thought about herself too, her own pain and darkness, her father's greed, her mother floating in the river, the years of hiding behind make-up and tattoos and shame, a victimhood that was scattered across her face alongside a constellation of piercing scars. She had enough self-absorbed hatred for the I's to litter the pages, and the jar would easily be replenished. All the jars would be full after today's gathering.

Finally, when her mental diatribe had exhausted itself, she pulled off the pads and took the damp glossy pages out of the printer, laying them out for the clean black print to dry. Every surface in the flat was covered with paper, across the kitchen table, along the sofa cushions, across the floors in every room. In the morning they'll be ready to be stripped and sorted, the most labour-intensive part of the process that left her with an aching back and shooting pains in her neck and shoulders.

But for now, she got undressed and showered the muck of the city from her body, letting the warm water wash away any last remnants of hatred. She wrapped a towel around herself and returned to the bedroom, taking a final look out the bedroom window. There was someone standing in the shadows of the doorway to the porn shop across the road. Just a cheapskate perv, she hoped, wanting to jack off to the faded skin-images in the window. She was too tired to think about who else it might be.

She sank into bed and fell asleep quickly, her mind empty and depleted, but full of the dark holes from where the words had been pulled.

Alexandra looked at the clock on the wall and noted with impatience that her client was five minutes late. A woman named Kira Lox whose sister was a good client, so she resolved to be patient.

She polished the counter one more time and retrieved the box from beneath it, anticipating this woman would be a smoker like her sister. She laid out the packets of papers of varying grades, several bundles of filters and the box of carrier leaves, and turned to double check that the jars lining the shelves above the cabinet behind her were full and gleaming.

Of course they were. She was nothing if not fastidious. The best way to stay on the straight-and-narrow, Adjei taught her some time ago, was to give full and complete commitment to something other than what was pushing you off the rails. From the moment she first met him in a bar in the factory district, he'd shown her acceptance and kindness. And he'd given her a blend to smoke, which helped her to believe there was hope for a new kind of life.

The buzzer rang and she looked at the small CCTV monitor hidden in the corner of the counter to see a young woman with black curtains of hair, her face glinting with piercings, eyes framed with black kohl.

"Oh great," she muttered, "a goth."

Alexandra buzzed her in and watched the woman push open the heavy gate that led into the alleyway, wondering if she'd notice the echoes of her own piercings, the pale scars on her lip and nose, the dents up her ears and along her cheekbones. She pulled down her sleeves to cover her tattoos.

She met Kira at the door and instantly knew this was going to be a tough one. Her gaze was direct and hateful, but there was sadness there too, her cheeks drawn as though she'd forgotten how to eat. Loss emanated from her like a pungent perfume, one that couldn't be washed away no matter how much hot water and soap was used.

"Come through," she said, leading her into the consulting room and walking behind the counter. "You found me ok?"

"Eventually." Her voice had a hardness that matched the aggression of her make-up. Alexandra hoped there was enough desperation inside her to soften any deep-rooted beliefs she may have. The blends need some space around certainty to reach consciousness level.

"Hopefully we'll be legal one day," she said, "and then I'll have a shop front. People will be able to open the door and walk straight in."

"And tell you what's hurting them?"

"Yes," Alexandra said. "Sometimes."

Kira nodded and said, "I want to forget that my sister is dead."

"Jennifer?" Alexandra stared at her, fingertips pressing onto the counter. "But... I only saw her a few months ago. She's dead?" Jennifer had been a client for a few years, a quiet young woman who suffered with anxiety and a whole host of fears. Crowds, spiders, water, germs. They all filled her with dread and crippled her daily life. But the blends were helping and she was going out more, she'd even met a woman in a bar and begun dating again.

"What happened?" she asked.

Kira shook her head. "I want this pain to go away." Her voice was low, exhausted with grief.

Alexandra nodded, recognising her sense of urgency, the overwhelming need for some kind of relief.

"Did Jennifer tell you how it works?" she asked.

"Yes, but..." Kira fiddled with the silver stud in her lower lip. The skin there was inflamed and Alexandra imagined her sitting on her couch at home, staring into the space of her sister's death and turning and turning the silver stud, the only movement her mind could manage. "She said it's just like smoking a regular roll-up, but... it still sounds weird. Like it's got to be dangerous, you know? There's got to be side-effects."

"It is a bit of a head fuck, for sure," she said. "The first thing to decide is your statement, and everything else flows from there. Get your statement right and the words will infuse into your neural pathways more effectively. It's like therapy multiplied by a hundred," she said, Kira nodding her understanding. "So, think about what you want to believe. Be precise and be particular. I'll make up the letters, enough for a month to begin with. If you don't smoke, you could take the letters in warm milk, not quite as effective but easier on the lungs."

"Smoking is fine," she said.

"So, what do you want your statement to be?"

Kira pulled her bottom lip into her mouth so her tongue could run over the cool ball of the stud. When she let it go, her lip was glistening with saliva. "I want... I want this pain to go away. I want my sister to still be alive." She looked at Alexandra in an accusatory way which made her feel defensive and a little angry, emotions she could use the next time she was wired up to the Wernicke machine.

"If you believe your sister is alive, you'll be looking for her constantly, wondering where she is, why she isn't returning your calls."

Kira frowned. "Ok, then, maybe I want to believe I never had a sister in the first place."

"I don't think you really want that."

"What the fuck do you know? You don't know me." Her anger escalated and her lips pulled into a sneer that seemed to be directed at the whole world, at her sister and herself, but it only lasted for a moment and Alexandra felt the tides of her own grief alongside Kira's, the undercurrents and crashing waves, the whirlpools and undulating weight of its vastness. She understood the mask of goth make-up and piercings were something to hide behind, retreat into some other place where she felt safe.

"It's ok," Alexandra said, "the blend is often the most difficult part. But it's worth getting it right. Trust me."

When she was doing her training with Adjei, he made her smoke a bad blend just so she could see what it was like. She used the statement *I want to get the fuck out of my life,* a sentiment that still felt close and raw, even now. But back then, she spent the days after the smoke feeling increasingly disconnected with a growing sense that she didn't belong, not on the streets, not in her local cafe, and then not even in her own flat. She'd become a paranoid wreck with even more anxiety than when she'd walked over the bridge and left her rich life behind. She knew then that she had to respect the words and the truth of their meaning, every letter and punctuation mark that went into the blend.

"Tell me how you're feeling right now," Alexandra said.

"Nervous. Angry. Scared." She turned the ball on her lip, again and again so her words came out muffled, but then her hand dropped and she said, "Jennifer had been talking about it for months, but I didn't think... I didn't know she really meant it, that she... hated her life enough to walk to the fucking tram and lie down on the tracks."

"Jennifer committed suicide?" Alexandra whispered, her voice breaking with the jolt of her mother's sudden presence. Not the gentle mother, but the woman so full of dark emptiness that she couldn't bear to live any more. Couldn't even bear the consolation of her only daughter.

"You want to know how I'm feeling right now?" Kira said, "I'm fucking angry that she didn't come to me that night, didn't trust me to help her. I'm angry and confused and fucking lost like when we were kids. I don't believe anything will make me feel better cos nothing can change what she did and nothing can bring her back. Whatever drug I smoke or swallow, it won't make a fuck load of difference." When she finally stopped, she was out of breath, her rage dissipating into a kind of defeat. "But before she did it, she told me about you, about... smoking words. She told me it helped her to feel better. Even though in the end... she did what she did."

Alexandra felt Kira's loss as her own failure. She must have given Jennifer the wrong blend, or the dose was too weak or infrequent. Or maybe the urban myths weren't myths after all. *Fuck.*

She inhaled slowly, forcing herself to concentrate and push back to what she knew to be true. "The blend doesn't just create a state change," Alexandra said. "You absorb the letters, the words, the meaning into your bloodstream so your mind can read it and build new neural pathways. It embeds your new truth into the physicality of your mind *and* your belief system at the same time. It's the ultimate in holistic treatments."

Kira looked sceptical.

"You believe that I want to help you, don't you?"

"I guess."

"And you don't believe I'm going to hurt you."

She took a step back but then laughed, quick and sharp. "Not intentionally."

"You've told your mind that I'm here to help and your mind believes it. If you told your mind that I might hurt you, I'd look different to you right now. *You'd* be different right now. Everything we see is subjective, filtered through our believe system. Belief is truth."

"Jennifer said some of the letters are stronger than others, that I should go for potent ones if I can."

"The z's, x's and q's are the most powerful due to their scarcity. The vowels are your everyday strength, essential to the blend but light, fragrant." Alex turned to the shelves and took down a jar of e's that she'd refilled from yesterday's gathering.

She unscrewed the lid and turned the jar at a tilt so Kira could see the letters tumbling over themselves within the smoky brown glass. They tumbled and tangled, getting caught in each other's loop as though they were playing. "Smell them," she said.

Kira leaned forward and breathed in the unmistakeable scent. "It's like bluebells," she said.

"The accuracy of the blend is the most important thing," she said. "I once had a couple who'd had a miscarriage. They wanted the blend *We never had a zygote*, just for the extra kick of a z. The y and g have got some heat too. I tried to put them off but they insisted, wouldn't take no for an answer. They came back a month later. In reality, they didn't think of their baby as a zygote or a foetus, so their minds didn't believe it. Their pain was still there, if anything it was worse because they'd been running away from it for so long." That was in the early days of Alexandra's practice, before she understood that helping people to lie to themselves wasn't the best use of her time. "Don't think about the letters," she said to Kira, "they all have their own unique properties. It's how you bring them together that gives them power. How truthful they are."

"All I ever wanted was for my sister to understand how spectacular she was. How much she was loved. I wanted her to be happy, free of the shit that went on in her head."

"Do you believe that she's happy now, wherever she is?"

Kira thought for a moment. "You mean I can't take it away? I can't make myself believe it never happened?"

"You can try. But in my experience, it won't help. You'll know you're being lied to and your mind will find a fuck load of ways to bring it to your attention. Truth is better."

Kira looked down at her ringed fingers resting on the counter, slender, with bitten nails and chipped black nail varnish, hands that knew the touch of her sister's skin, hands that likely threw flowers into her grave.

"What's the last blend you gave her?" Kira asked.

"I... I don't remember."

"Can you find out?"

Alexandra nodded, playing along in the hope that it might help her to understand, or at least give her some comfort. She pulled out the ledger from beneath the counter, ran her finger down the pages in search of Jennifer's name. When she found it, there was a list of five blends that Alexandra had made up for her.

"The last was to help her overcome her fear of water," Alexandra said. "The statement was *I want to dive into the ocean*. She thought that if she believed it enough, she'd be able to do it, and then she'd have conquered her fear. Desire is a good approach."

Kira's fingers twitched like she had electricity jumping through her veins. "After I identified her body," she said, "I went to her flat and found the butt of the last cigarette she rolled. She didn't smoke all the letters. She left some in the fabric wrapping. I saw them. They were black and hard. A v, a couple of o's and t's, a c and an n. She didn't smoke I want to dive into the ocean. She smoked I want to die."

Alexandra stared at her, the truth of Kira's words thudding through her with more force than rage could ever muster. "I... I was trying to help her," she said. She felt her voice to be a distant whisp of wind, something inconsequential, irrelevant and disappearing into the distance.

"You had a duty of care," Kira said, her voice breaking and tears streaming down her face. "You didn't even think about the consequences of what you gave her. You just took her money and sent her away with the very thing that would give her enough courage to kill herself."

"No... no... it's not like that. I wouldn't...'

"But you did."

Kira wiped the tears from her cheeks with the heal of her hand, the black kohl of her eyes smeared across her skin to give her a menacing glare, and Alexandra realised that it was Kira who had been watching her, waiting for the moment to confront her. It was Kira loitering in the shop doorway last night.

"I wanted you to know what happened," Kira said, "that's all. I want you to know how you're messing with people's heads. Fucking people up."

Kira turned away from the counter and walked to the door, but Alexandra could feel that her fear and longing stayed put at the counter, as though her body had taken the steps but her soul had stayed behind, refusing to leave. Kira paused at the door, her fingertips resting on the handle.

Alexandra said, "My sister is full of peace and tranquillity. She is love, and she is free."

Kira didn't move but Alexandra could hear her breath deepening.

"Does that sound like the truth, Kira?"

Kira turned and looked at Alexandra, fresh tears falling from her eyes.

"Let me do this for you," she said. "It will be a gift."

Kira watched as Alexandra turned to the shelves and took down the necessary letter and punctuation jars, lining them up along the counter.

She opened up four soft linen cloths the colour of milk, opened the first jar and took a scoop of u's, letting two drop onto each square of linen, their soft little bodies glistening black like the pared wings of a beetle.

She repeated the process with the other letters, finally finishing with the r's that would imbue *sister, tranquillity* and *free* with their special resonance. She felt all the letters as living beings, albeit dormant at present, each one holding the possibility of meaning. They were the living potential of Kira's change and healing, and she wondered, briefly, if the same was possible for herself.

Kira stepped up to the counter and gazed down at the tangled letters. "They're beautiful," she said, breathing in their multifaceted fragrance, like earthenware pots that had been heated in the midday sun and then rained on. Washed flowers. Poppy heads, gardenias and torn leaves. All of life was there, in that little pile of tangled truth.

Alexandra folded the corners together of three of the squares to make small bundles that she tied with a piece of green string.

"Smoke one a week," she said, "and don't be tempted to smoke them sooner. It takes time for the mind to absorb a new reality and truly believe it. Habits of behaviour create habits of mind, and that's what creates belief." She held a cigarette paper, placed a filter at one end and sprinkled a layer of carrier leaves, then took the contents of the final linen square and sprinkled them over the top. "Make sure you get the letters even," she said, "a steady thread of inhalation that your mind can reassemble." She pressed the letters gently to mingle with the leaves. They were soft and smooth to the touch, somewhere between rubber and plastic, even though they comprise entirely of natural ink. She rolled the cigarette deftly, licked and secured its edge, twisting the end and holding it out for Kira, whose dark-kohled eyes were now edged with curiosity.

"Smoke it after dinner tonight, perhaps. Choose a time when your mind is open to new possibilities. Most people prefer to be relaxed, mellow. I've also heard of people who smoke when they're a bit afraid. Fuck knows how they do that, watching horror films or something. When you're afraid, your mind opens right up, fight or flight, you're alert, looking for danger."

"I think I'll go for mellow," Kira said. She watched Alexandra make up a package for her, the linen bundles and smoking paraphernalia neatly tucked into a small cardboard box that she nestled into an unmarked paper bag. It could hold a sandwich from the deli or a new paperback from the bookshop. Another way that she kept her wares flying under the radar.

"You know how to get in touch if you want more," Alexandra said.

Kira took the bag and Alexandra came around from behind the counter to open the door for her, leading her out into the alleyway and letting her through the security gate, locking it behind her.

Kira looked back at her through the bars and Alexandra could see an openness that wasn't there when she arrived. Maybe her hard edges have blurred enough for the smoke to seep through, Alexandra hoped.

They nodded goodbye to each other, and back in the shop Alexandra began the routine of tidying up but she felt dizzy, her legs weak, her breath shallow, and she sank to the floor, leaning against the cabinet and resting her head in her hands. She felt overwhelmed with the feeling that nothing would change for people like Jennifer and Kira, that the world and everyone in it was destined for annihilation and the only weapon used would be millions of minds believing in anger and hatred. Inside her own mind was no better. She could feel her own well-worn grooves of rage and guilt and loss, as deep and permanent as the tram tracks outside her door.

She couldn't remember the last time she made up a statement for herself. At what point did she feel she didn't need it anymore? She hadn't seen Adjei for over a year and she struggled to recall his voice, the lessons he gave her on mentation and how to live a good life. He saved her from spiralling self-destruction, but instead she'd isolated herself into slow and insidious decline, city life and shame infecting her thoughts every day, all embedded by the weekly gathering of mentations. She'd become like a doctor that didn't have faith in her own cure.

Grief welled up inside her as powerful as the day her mother died, but it slid into a gathering sensation that her mother was there beside her, a presence she hadn't allowed herself to feel for many years. She closed her eyes to absorb it, felt her mother's love and goodness surrounding her, breathed in her vanilla scent and the touch of her hair against her cheek. She knew this warmth and comfort was transient, but she could feel her mind loosening, small pockets of space opening up where before there was dense despair. When she opened her eyes again, there was an unexpected brightness in the room.

Alexandra pushed herself up and pulled a piece of paper and a pen from the drawer and placed it on the counter. She stared at the creamy page, felt the blank moment before the words formulated their meaning in her mind. She searched for who she was, what she was, and as the words came she scribbled them down. *Angry. Fearful. Hiding. Dogged. Bitter.* She let them flow and enjoyed this different kind of accumulated language, a process that felt less invasive than the Wernicke machine, felt almost therapeutic. When she'd emptied her mind of all the bad things she thought of herself, she wrote a new list of their opposites, words that filled her with a sense of her mother's lightness, her openness.

Two lists. Two different people. She drew a box around the words of the person she was now and struck lines across them, over and over again until the words were barely legible. She stared at what remained. Words that felt impossible. Abstract and naively hopeful. She tried to formulate them into a statement but her mind was tired, as if the energy required for any more thought would tip her into dark oblivion. Instead, she accepted what she had on the page. Words that might be the start of something, she thought, a new way of being, perhaps.

She fetched a variety of jars from the shelves which she lined up on the counter. She measured out letters and punctuation onto a piece of fabric and wrapped it into a bundle. She craved the instant hit of a smoke but instead she went upstairs to the kitchen, poured milk into a pan, tipped in the letters and turned on the hob, stirring the draught with a wooden spoon. The black letters and punctuation turned and tumbled in the paper-white of the milk, and when a gentle steam started to lift she poured it into a glass and swallowed it down in a series of gulps, the letters stroking her throat. She wiped her mouth with the back of her hand, the words already buzzing through her system as though she'd inhaled them, as though there was a vast hole inside herself waiting to absorb the thing she'd resisted for so long.

She wandered into the living room and glanced out the window, the night drawing the street into a cloaked version of itself, the streetlamps barely reaching the pavements so all she could see were shadowy figures and the occasional tram trundling past. In the bedroom she pulled the blinds and lay on the bed. The milk dispersed meaning through her mind and in response her body buzzed with a sense of shift, something slow and indefinable, its destination unknown. She didn't try to control it, instead allowed its passage through her synapses, the Wernicke and Broca regions of her brain opening to accept this new language of truth.

She felt the blankets and pillows like a cocoon encasing her body, and a vision rose up in her consciousness – the square screen of the Wernicke machine, and inside, the faded tattoo that covered her arm. As she watched, the cleaning solution swirled and bubbled, the ink drifting and gathering, as though tasting the skin and the shapes and this different kind of ink. Slowly the liquid ink began to coalesce, the tattooed shapes filling with movement and Alexandra smiled as she saw the ink solidify into bees and butterflies, flowers and fluttering birds, the grey lines teeming with caterpillars and beetles.

She watched in wonder as the curious creatures explored their new home, her mind sinking deeper into her longed-for truth. Outside, two cats howled and hissed at each other, and she felt herself to be a breathing instrument within a vast city orchestra of intention and belief.

In the distance, sirens started up to join the nightly concert.

Sally Gander is a writer and Creative Writing teacher. Her nonfiction has appeared in *Hinterland, Litro,* and *The Lincoln Review* and has been nominated for the Pushcart Prize. She has taught on the prestigious Creative Writing program at Bath Spa University, and currently teaches at the Open University and Advanced Studies in England. You can read more of her published work at https://sallymgander.blog/publications/. Instagram: @sallygander68

Operative 38XY Completes The Stint

by Finola Scott

I'm proud to be the one selected
though this blue planet is strange.
I was taught of gravity, black holes
no mention of pollution or poverty.
But so many wonders of rock and air.

Seven years since I cloaked in pink

I've tholed it, collected samples,
studied these hairy sweating creatures.
I noted ice and species vanishing.
At last my time is up. Soon in starlight
this borrowed flesh will dissolve in ocean.

Seven years since I first felt loam

I will cast off this frail frame, discard
heavy bones, unreliable organs, strange habits.
My human swears he tastes sea in my hair.
He says I am music, calls me Siren, thinks
me Selkie. I shall gift him this pelt of fur.

Finola Scott's poems scatter on the wind landing in such places as *The High Window, New Writing Scotland, Gutter* and *Lighthouse*. She has 3 pamphlets published, for info visit Finola Scott Poems FB. She enjoys feeding grandchildren and blue-tits, not necessarily at the same time.

Our Generation, We Were The People With Wings

by Elizabeth Scott Tervo

Soon we knew how to genetically engineer ourselves
and we went fluttering about on butterfly wings
or eagle wings, or bat wings, from pale blue to rich purple
or whatever color you chose from the palette provided.

The wings were innervated into our existing systems
so we could easily send electric impulses down from the brain,
out the spinal roots, to the horizontal rootlets,
branching to the plump feathered muscles
to pull and push the air away
and we could fly.
At night they were warm to cuddle under.

For decades we went, skimming the treetops, startling the birds
until they realized we weren't birds of prey.
We flew for delight, travel, and commuting, not hunting,
though you could get a license to take a falcon on your wrist
if you wanted.

Then we began to grow old.

For some of us, our wings stopped working first
and we fell out of the blue.
For others, our wings were the last thing to fail
and, without memory, we lived on in care facilities

where kind attendants held a soft rope to our ankle
as we glided in slow circles over a padded garden.
Or we lay in bed on one side, incurious, one wing idly flapping.
We don't know which part of us will still be alive tomorrow.

Sometimes I think I'll organize a forest for us:
One by one we'll say goodbye, take a final dose of morphine, fly
our last flight over the leaves, failing slowly, slowly
and crashing silently dead in the woods.
I say 'silently' because there will be nobody to hear us.
Later the kind attendants will look for us
and find us and bury us.
I'll call it 'The Forest of Silence'.
Other times I think I'll leave the manner of my passing
for my children to decide.
And sometimes I think I'll leave it up to God.

Elizabeth Scott Tervo's poetry has been published in *Ruminate, Eye to the Telescope,* and the *Wheel,* and won a prize at Inscape in 2022. She co-coordinates the Doxacon Seattle writers group for Speculative Literature and Christianity. Her memoir about the country of Georgia on the eve of its independence was published in 2021 in Georgian translation and sold out its initial run.

The Dragon Raids
by Brian M. Milton

The dragon raided us again today, but she missed the most important of we and did not take any stores. It is strange that she raids our shelter so often at this time of year. She has seen how our stores are low this early in the summer so must know there is nothing to steal. The dragons have beset us for hundreds of years but still, their ways are difficult to understand.

This time the dragon used a lot of smoke. She lifted the top off our shelter, letting the sun burn into the darkness and set panic amongst the elements of our whole. She blew her smoke into the centre, trying to blow elements to the side and expose the core where we keep the young. The new elements cowered, too young to listen to the calming song the centre of the whole sang. But the dragon never appears to be very interested in the majority of the young.

She pulls out the sections of the shelter they are growing in and holds them to the light for her own reasons, turning them back and forth, but she is not like a raiding bird who wants to dig out the young and eat them. The dragon only looks quickly, for she is only interested in the special, bigger, elements of ourself.

A healthy whole must always be strong and ready. Plenty of stores safely tucked away for the coming winter and always producing more and more elements. But unless we want to live and build on the outside of the shelter we must be ready to leave to find a new dwelling, and to leave a new, smaller, whole behind. The dragon does not want this to happen. She wants all the elements to stay where she can control them and raid our stores when they get full.

Sometimes she will fool the elements by creating more space in the

100

shelter and sometimes she will even split us in two, forcing us to create a new central element for the new whole that is without one. That is traumatic, elements of a whole, body and mind, split across two shelters, not knowing which is the correct one, pulled away from the central song and forced to fall back on dumb instinct to create the new central element of a mind, not from the best candidate but from the soonest available. But, if we are clever and use our elements to hide a new central element, then, just perhaps, we can escape from the dragon's slavery and fly free in search of a new home, one where dragons do not harass us.

There are tales, handed down through the memory of the successive minds, of times when many of us used to live in trees. Dry, warm holes, easily defended from the birds and the wasps and somewhere that a dragon could not fit. In those days the smoke meant a fire and we had to be prepared to flee to a new tree. But then the dragons learned to fool us by blowing their smoke where there is no fire.

Dragons are very strange creatures. They enslave us and force us to live in their shelters and raid us of so much of our stores but we cannot understand how they do this. They act in an intelligent manner, controlling us, but they are clearly only one creature. How can just one creature, on its own, be so clever? It takes thousands of individual elements, working together, to be clever - the maids, the guards, the foragers and the central, larger, element combining to create intelligence. How is it possible that a single creature like a dragon could possibly act as if they are thinking? Many elements of the whole can act together, combining to defend the shelter, in a way that no single element could. If only we were not raided so often, perhaps we could find time to understand.

This time the dragon was not so clever. As she blew her smoke, causing the elements that were made stupid by being too far from the central song to think that a fire was coming and they must flee, the central element's song pulled most of us together. The closer we came, the cleverer we became. We manoeuvred the maids and the guards, even some of the stupid males, to cluster around the chamber where the young element we had selected was lying. Because the young element becomes so much bigger when she becomes a central element, the chamber she lies in is different from the others. But we moved and danced and shuffled and jostled around it, milling amongst the smoke the dragon had blown, confusing her so she could not see and, despite being lifted high in the air and turned from side to side in the strong light of the guiding sun, we kept moving and eventually the dragon returned us to the centre and lifted the next section of our shelter. She took each in turn, but we kept dancing and waggling so all sections looked the same and, eventually, the dragon worked her way through all the sections and replaced the shelter top.

As soon as the top was returned, and it was dark once more we clustered around the centre again where we are at our most intelligent. The young central element larvae were untouched and no parts of us had been removed to another shelter. We had succeeded in fooling the dragon this time, she had not seen how we filled the shelter and how all was prepared.

The time has come, we have grown large enough to become two. The old central element of our whole and her foragers will fly out of the shelter at the height of the sun and find a new real home, far from the dragon, and we will become they and we, or we and they, and one of us will find that perfect tree in which to create their new home. We will escape. To live in freedom once more, foraging far and wide amongst the flowers and trees and splitting time and again, becoming many, many they, and perhaps, in time, there will be enough of us that we will come to study and understand the dragons and one day, when we understand them fully, we can free our sisters from their slavery.

Brian lives on the edge of Glasgow beside several beehives, which, he is convinced are giving him the evil eye. When not hiding from flying insects, he is a member of the Glasgow Science Fiction Writer's Circle and has been lucky to have short fiction published in places such as *Shoreline of Infinity* and *New Maps*.
These days he can be found shouting at the internet on Mastodon
@munchkinstein @mastodon.scot

Cop 27
by GW Colkitto

Meant to reassure   as friendly as   PC 49
    solving crimes with a quip and a smile

    but no-one believes   the voices saying
it's not too late   only getting close   like an asteroid
       seen   and tracked

      and like the asteroid
we always have the nuclear   option
blast   and hope   the dead are not
        us or

is it and us

      asteroids might have an armed response
        bigger better
    so we
  if survivors   are enslaved

did I tell you
      lands   are drowned
not tomorrow
     yesterday
        do you see hands

a child   an old man   yours?

waving   waving   as lives   slip   under   or
stretching from a desert   withered   marching hours to
        drink piss   warped news
wrapped   in plastic shrouds   to k e e p t h e m

                    wholesome

  must not   pollute   oceans   ice   b e w a r e b u r n i n g
forests

        the never-born will never see but

            when new life comes to Earth

the ones we cannot imagine   will they resurrect our bones

hold in a glass case   type Homo Sapiens
        believed extinct but if any   linger around
                        kill on sight

George Colkitto writes for the pleasure of words. He was born, brought up and lives in Paisley, Scotland. An ex-Inspector of Taxes, Chartered Account, and bookshop owner, he writes both poetry and prose. He has read at Bloody Scotland, Aye Write, The Thames River Festival, Scottish Writers Centre, Paisley Museums and Art Galleries and in venues from Newcastle to Nairn.

Eels

by Clint Wastling

I'll row you to the Isle of Llanddwyn
there you'll find which love to nurture.
Consult the white witch Dwynwen,
her talking eels reveal the future.

Silver eels with a metallic sheen
I've seen them enroute for the Sargasso Sea.
Intent on experiencing brine,
Their inseparable love will tell what yours will be.

Pick up the eels! the witch demanded.
As he did they coiled around his arms.
They are blessed and cursed to know the truth
But truth shifts like a witch's charms.

Clockwise you love a man,
Counter-clockwise a woman
But if they draw blood —
You're mine, you are mine!
This augury is now complete
And that which was yours is now forfeit.

Your head will rest on pillows of rock
As green as the emerald sea.
Skin and sinew will turn to stone
And here you'll wait eternity.

Eternity as stone until a lover's kiss
Releases you from where you lie;
And on the fair Isle of Llanddyyn
perhaps you'll love and live again before you die.

Clint Wastling's poetry has been widely published. His first collection of poetry is entitled *Layers* (Maytree Press). His novel, *Tyrants Rex,* is a fantasy set some 3000 years in the future and is published by Stairwell Books.

A Prophet In His Own Country
by Lynden Wade

From a crow's nest, you can see everything.

When I first hatched, high up in the topmost branches of a tree, all I was aware of was food and the way the nest swayed with the wind. But as the four of us chicks grew, we'd look down at the world laid out beneath us, forest and field, scurrying beasts and swooping birds. Maybe that is why crows are augurs, fortune tellers: we can see so much further than other creatures.

Yes, my fledgelings. I want you to listen carefully, and learn from my story. I did not want to be an augur when I was young. I wanted to sing. I listened to the blackbird on the nearest cottage's rooftop, his molten notes trickling into the evening light, and saw how the human creatures would pause in their drudging walk and look up, worry lifting from their faces for a moment.

Not long after I had left the nest, I sat in a bush by a path and began my song. Something erupted from my throat, jagged and raucous. I tried to soften it, but it came out louder still. Nor could I make it skip up and down. A child playing nearby threw a stone at me. I darted to one side, but it grazed my wing. A linnet watching me laughed.

I flew back to my nest with bruises on my body and pride.

My father refused my demand to snap the linnet's head off. "The gods made the linnet to sing," he said. "And the blackbird. Our calling is to warn. It is a gift to be proud of."

And it is true that as I reached maturity I heard things other birds could not, sharp though the hearing is of all feathered things.

The first time was when I stopped by a dead body in the ditch, some way out of the village. I'd known the man: he'd been a pedlar, a regular visitor bringing items from far away. The last time I'd seen him, he stumbled up this very road heading for the village, shivering and vomiting and finally collapsing by the roadside. No one had moved his body, and on the third day, I began to peck here and there.

I'd just ripped off the first tasty morsel when the approach of a group made me fly into the tree above. I gulped down my bite as I watched from above. A woman led, with a clutch of children shuffling behind. They would pass in a minute and then I could carry on with my meal.

To my irritation, she stopped. She stared at the body a while, then bent to search it. First, she drew out some shining discs, which she pushed into a slit in her garments. The children watched with dull eyes. Human eyes are always dull compared to birds' eyes, and much more so when hungry. They were all scrawny and as ragged as a mangy dog. But a spark flickered in their faces as the woman drew a large packet out of the pedlar's bag. Mumbles rose as they huddled around to watch her unwrap and distribute it, then scurried down the road, jaws working.

At that moment, I realised that the mumbling came not from the children but from my stomach. This was not just a churning, but a voice. I did not know the word it kept repeating. Cholera? But the pedlar knew it, and his flesh warned me: "Death – disease! Spread by food! Tell the children!"

I flew ahead of them and perched on a fence to caw my warning. I received a flick of a glance from one child who turned back to tearing at the food in his hand. The rest of the band was engrossed in pushing hunks down their throats.

I lifted myself off the fence and flapped round the woman's head. She waved her hand at me and passed another piece of the food to the littlest child. Desperate, I dived at the bread to snatch it from them. The woman beat me away with a burst of animal fury, hissing through her teeth.

What could I do? I flew off to peck at my feathers and restore my sleek looks.

The next day a terrible stench led me to the family, who sprawled under a hedge on the other side of the village. Three children lay lifeless round the woman's feet. She held the last in her arms, despite its wet, stinking wrappings, but death was in both their faces, and she suddenly jerked forward to retch. As she wiped her mouth, she looked into the baby's face, sighed and crumpled. Now everyone lay quite still.

Why had they not listened? The voice inside me had spoken true. How stupid the woman had been!

Well, I would not be discouraged. I launched myself into the sky to survey the land from above.

A smell in the air tickled my nostrils and little eddies of wind tickled my feathers. The weather was changing. I circled to try to work it out and a whisper began in my head that got louder and louder until it was a shriek. "Storm! Storm!"

It was going to be a bad one, I could tell. Trees would come down and ships would be lost. As yet, the creatures below me saw no sign of it. I knew it was my work to warn everyone.

The birds and the beasts listened. They took flight or buried themselves deep in their lairs. The cows and horses in the fields grew skittish. A few of the older villagers muttered at the strange behaviour of their animals, but only to themselves. The one person to stop and listen was a woman who lived on her own. She looked over to her neighbour, who was coming home from the field.

"Don't go out tonight, Tom," she said. "Storm coming. Bad 'un. Ye don't want to be treading those paths through the wood on a night like this."

The man frowned. "This some strange way of warning me about the Customs Men, Biddy? Sky's clear as a new handkerchief."

"No, Tom. No. I don't interfere with the Gentlemen. I'm just telling ye what the Crow said."

"Crow said, eh?" The man scowled further. "Don't let Schoolmaster hear ye say that. He says we should be moving out of the Dark Ages now."

The woman whimpered a little, but the man stomped into his house.

I had done my work, but my warning had been heeded by only one villager. I flew through the dusk to find shelter. There was an ancient castle to the south, a crumbled ruin but still with half a tower standing. I jostled and fought with other birds large and small for a space until, with a splatter of rain and a howling of wind, the storm began. Then we waited, huddled close.

At dawn it blew out and we could spread and shake ourselves. I went back to the village to see what havoc the storm had brought.

Trees lay sprawled across ditches and clearings, their roots splayed at the sky like claws. Further on I flew over the fields, the wheat flattened and scattered.

The woman — Biddy, wasn't that her name? — was on her doorstep, peering out nervously. Next door's chimney lay in pieces round the side. Vegetable gardens were flattened, roofs smashed in. Biddy's garden patch was a sodden ruin.

Out from Tom's house came a woman balling one fist in the other, face all twisted.

"He's not come home," she called to Biddy. "I woke up and he wasn't there. He never come back. Dan and George said they'd go back and look for him. Said they'd been caught in the storm and run home, thought Tom was just behind 'em."

Biddy was looking the other way, where a pair of men emerged from the woods, heads hanging low. They tugged at the bridle of a pony and it came on reluctantly. Over its back was a motionless man.

The woman who had spoken to Biddy ran up to them. "No, no, no..." She lifted the man's face from where it bumped against the horse's flank, touching, listening, shaking the shoulders. A moan leaked out of her, grew into a wail. "Tom! My Tom! What happened to him?"

"Tree fell on him, Mary," said one of the men. "We found him under a beech, all his bones broke."

They took him off the pony's back and carried him towards his house. I could see from my rooftop that his leg flopped round like a fish and his side was as red and raw as crushed berries. He would have made a tasty meal in a day or two, but he was taken inside and I would not be able to get to him.

Biddy moved over to Tom's woman hesitantly and laid a hand on her arm. Tom's woman shook it off. "Don't touch me! You foresaw this. You witch!"

"Hoi," I shouted, "it was me who warned you, not her! And if you'd listened, Tom would still be alive. Fools!"

They certainly were fools. From that day no one would talk to Biddy. They only gave her cold stares or muttered to one another. Now her shoulders hunched and her head drooped: humans are best in flocks, not solitary. She began talking to us birds in her little vegetable patch out of sheer loneliness. That was how I first knew she was going to bear a child; but when her belly grew big, the villagers saw too and whispered to each other about it. Her husband had gone to sea, they said, but wasn't that six months ago, in the autumn? Someone said it was three months, but that person was soon silenced. Six months, they were sure; so the child must be witch-spawn.

And that is why, when she was ready to give birth, she was all alone. Her whimpers drifted across to me in my bush and kept me awake that night, turning into moans and groans and shrieks. I cannot understand why humans do not adopt our way of giving birth. Their way is undignified, dirty and dangerous; and it killed Biddy. I suppose the child died too, trapped inside. It was days before someone went in to find out what had happened to her — the curate a man new to the village — and his entrance into the cottage was followed by much head-shaking from the locals.

I was disgusted with the whole village. I had grown to respect Biddy as the one person in the community with ears, and I left her corpse untouched out of respect. I decided I would forget being an augur. I would be a creature of this age, like the Schoolmaster, and ignore any more messages.

But a new voice was pulling at me already, from the new-dug field at the far end of the village. As the first crops grew, the new shoots whispered.

They murmured with one voice, calling a name over and over: "Annie, Annie!" The longing that hung in the wheat heads crawled up the stalks from the roots, fed from the soil below.

Who was Annie, anyway? I ignored the voice all through the growing season. When the wheat was harvested and taken away, I thought I'd have peace at last. Only for a moon cycle, though. Just before the next sowing, the farmer made a man from fistfuls of the very straw that whispered and propped him up with a pole. Waves of sorrow rolled out from him, and he murmured and muttered just like the wheat.

It was clear I needed to have a talk with him.

I hopped onto his shoulder. "Now, come along, my man," I said. "There's no point in going on. The folk around here are all dolts. I'm sorry to say no one is going to listen."

"Crow..." the straw man murmured. "At last. Crows are augurs."

I groaned inwardly. "You'd better tell me all, then."

"My sweetheart... not forsaken... oh, Annie!"

In broken phrases, he told me his story. How two brothers loved one girl. She made her choice, and the other brother killed his lucky rival in fury, then buried him in the newly dug field.

"Ah! You want me to peck out the murderer's eyes?" Maybe this was my true calling – avenger. It sounded more promising than the thankless one of augur.

"No, no," he muttered. "Let me... finish."

Knowing Annie carried the dead brother's child, the murderer urged her to marry him, so the baby wouldn't be called a bastard. But the murdered man's spirit longed to reach the girl and the child, a longing which snaked through the soil, travelled up the roots and stems of the new growth, and lingered in the wheat even after it was cut.

"Oh, Crow, help! Help me! Talk to Annie. Tell her... didn't leave her."

"I'm not sure how that will help her," I objected.

"Might make... make her heart lighter," sighed the straw man.

The sweetheart lived in a tiny cottage on the other side of the village, easily located by the thin wailing of the child. Why do human children make that noise? It's not the lusty squawking of chicks needing feeding – it's a half-hearted discontent. I alighted on the windowsill and peered in. The child was in a wooden nest. A woman stirred a pot on the fire while rocking the baby with her foot. The child's wailing was dying down, the pauses between sobs growing longer. I waited patiently for it to stop, then opened my beak.

"Woman!" I proclaimed with authority. "You must not weep. Your lover did not desert you. He promises to watch over you and the child."

It suddenly struck me: what a foolish message! What use was a straw man to this pair?

It certainly did not comfort her.

"Shoo! Get away from her, you!" She flapped her apron at me.

I was a messenger of the gods. I was not frightened by aprons. I dug my claws in and repeated my story, lame as it sounded.

"Off! Don't wake the baby!" She picked up a broom and swiped it at me. Heavenly or not, I had to retreat. But only to the rooftop of the next cottage.

From there I saw a man enter. He had black hair, and muddy boots that he yanked off as soon as he got in.

"What, supper not ready yet?" He sounded irritated.

"Not long now, Joseph," said the woman. "It took a while to get the baby off to sleep."

"The baby again!" The man's voice rose. "Always the baby. I think you care more for the baby than me!"

I listened to him as he went on and on. As his rage grew, so did mine. How dared he? I should have been allowed to peck out the murderer's eyes after all, rather than bear stupid messages. Well, maybe someone else could bring justice. I raised my voice and shouted. I told his neighbours how the black-haired man had murdered his brother and stolen his girl. I called the man all the filthy names I could think of – first the basest names in bird language, then the foul names of man's language, that sound ugly even when uttered by a crow.

Someone was looking up at me in puzzlement. I could see he understood me and that he was surprised at this.

It was the curate. Since his arrival, he had spent much of his time touring the village, going in and out of the cottages. The villagers greeted him with increasing respect and warmth. He was often outdoors, too, in the woods, or over the downs, ears cocked to the wind. I'd wondered if he wished he were a bird. He certainly looked a little like a crow, with his black clothes and bright eyes.

"That's quite a story," he said to me. "Though your language, dear bird!"

At last, someone who would listen. "A true tale, your reverence. A murder that needs avenging. I trust you will see that justice is done?"

Yes, I know. That was not what the scarecrow had asked me to do. But the man with the muddy boots was abusing the woman. And he had stolen the straw man's child.

"Hmm, murder, eh?" murmured the curate. And to my astonishment, he smiled and shook his head.

Was he smiling at the thought of justice being done? The shake of the head did not fit. I thought I would follow him to see what he would do next.

He was going home. It was a mild evening and the windows in his house in the high street were ajar. I could perch on the sill and listen and watch. The curate was taking off his hat and coat and talking to a woman in an apron.

"Yes, thank you, Mrs Oats, a good day. Though I am questioning my decision to live alone. I am starting to imagine things."

Imagine things! I clacked my beak with irritation. The man was a disappointment.

The woman took away his hat and coat. The curate sat down at a little table in the corner and took out a feather. What was he going to do with that? One was hardly enough to fly with. Then he took something filled with black liquid, dipped the feather in it and pulled towards himself an item as white as the sheets that flap in people's gardens, but quite small. On it, he began to make stains. They wriggled over the page like worms, the feather making a scratching noise like a claw. He bent over this for quite some time. Mrs Oats banged food down beside him, which he pushed aside to continue with his work. Finally, he stopped, put down the feather and leaned back. He lifted the sheet and began to talk, all the while looking at the stains. And as he talked, he told the story of two brothers who loved one girl and how one murdered the other and buried his body in a field, only for the scarecrow to whisper to the girl that she was not deserted.

"So, Crow," he said suddenly, "I think I have it all down in writing now."

I had not realised he knew I was there. "Is writing what you call those scratches?"

His eyebrows shot up, and then he laughed. "I've been told before that my handwriting is execrable, but never yet by a crow."

"But what is the purpose of this writing of yours?" I hopped with impatience.

"As a record, dear Crow. So the story will be remembered for posterity."

"Excellent, excellent! I didn't think you were taking me seriously."

"I suppose you have many a tale to tell, Crow," he said with a smile.

I cocked my head to study his face. Was he mocking me? I hoped not. I liked this man.

"Oh, I do." I went on to tell him about the beggar woman and Biddy. He listened carefully. Mrs Oats came in to take away the food. She sniffed when she saw it had not been touched.

The curate had to light a candle before I'd ended my tale. When I'd finished, he picked up the feather again.

"I shall write it all down, Crow," he said. "I think I rather enjoy hearing voices after all."

I was not sure what he meant. But I was relieved that someone was listening to me again. And someone who was respected in the village, unlike poor Biddy. Surely he would tell someone else soon?

Besides, I enjoyed his company. This crow-man talked to me respectfully, as one of the gods' go-betweens to another. I became his regular companion as he went about his business in the following days, his coat flapping behind him like wings. Thus I witnessed his meeting in the street with Mr Gervase.

I knew this was a man of some authority. There was much bowing and pulling off of caps when he rode by. My hopes rose. My curate had decided to take the case to him! I could not hear what they were saying but noted they shook hands when they parted.

A few hours later I followed him up the high street. He was heading for the big house, where Mr Gervase lived. This was promising! My curate passed through the gates and up the long drive, only to appear again a minute later, walking into the garden at the back. Mr Gervase was taking a stroll with a young companion, who walked with difficulty, swinging himself along on two sticks under his arms.

"Ah, Foster!" said Mr Gervase. "Thank you for coming. You had a think about my proposition, then. Very grateful. Boy's been lacking a tutor for too long now."

"I wish I had gone to the village school!" the companion burst out.

Mr Gervase threw his head back and laughed. "The village school! All very well for cottagers and smiths and the like. Plain reading and writing and knowing your place. Not the education for the son of a landowner. No, no."

"Indeed, sir," said Mr Foster mildly. "If you yourself had known your place you would not have risen to where you are now."

Mr Gervase stared at him, then gave another shout of laughter. "True, true. This is the age of the entrepreneur. See you're not cowed by money and big houses. Robert, your new tutor, Mr Foster. May as well get acquainted now. I've papers to sign."

Left by themselves, the boy and the man looked awkward. Then the boy said, "I could have gone to the village school. My legs may not work, but I can get round with my crutches. And there is nothing wrong with my brain. But Father won't let me. I wish I could fly out of here, like that crow."

The curate looked round and saw me in the tree above. He did not seem very surprised. "Ah, the Crow! He follows me everywhere now. If you cannot fly out, he can fly in. He could tell you all about the world outside."

"If he could talk," said Robert gloomily.

"He does. And for our first lesson, I will tell you a story he told me."

My curate was going to tell my prophecies to a boy! Not the rector, not Mr Gervase, but a boy who could not walk. I almost flew away in disgust.

"Our first lesson will be now," commanded the boy.

"Very well."

The curate found them both a seat overlooking the garden. He told the boy the story of the beggar woman and the pedlar.

Robert listened, and when the tale had finished was silent for a while. Then he said, "But it is just a story?"

"If it is," the curate said, "there is a kernel of truth. Disease and poverty blight the lives of the poor."

"She should not have begged. She should have found honest work."

"There is not always work to be had. Machines are replacing workers in this day and age. And the workhouses break up families. Many would rather die than go to them for help."

Robert was quiet again. Then he demanded another story. Mr Foster told him of Biddy and how she was shunned, then the story of the two brothers. I flew down from the tree to perch on a stone figure nearby, the better to hear.

"That's terrible," Robert cried at the end. "The murderer should be apprehended at once. I will ask Father to see that justice is done."

"My boy, it is a fable, not a true event."

Fury filled my breast. I erupted from my branch, cawing and beating my wings.

Robert laughed and pointed at me. "Crow is angry that you doubt his word."

"The boy's right," I shouted.

"Dear me," said Mr Foster, "Robert, I think you are correct."

"So let's talk to Father!"

My curate chewed his lip. "You will need evidence."

"It's all in the story! We must dig in the corner of the new field."

I settled into a glide and landed on the stone figure once more, but could not help hopping with anticipation. Some action at last! The boy was on his feet already, pushing himself along the path on his sticks and calling for his father.

There was a good deal of arguing about this. Mr Gervase was at first incredulous that his son wanted to dig up a precious field because of a story. Then he started to fit the elements of the tale to recent events in the village. Yes, he'd heard that two brothers, William and Daniel, had been rivals for a girl called Annie. Everyone knew Annie had preferred William, and yet he'd suddenly disappeared the evening the common was dug up for a new field. Both the brothers had been involved in the work.

"Can't dig the whole field over," protested Mr Gervase. "Crops growing. A good year, this."

"Perhaps Crow will show us where to look?" The curate looked over at me with a little smile.

"I'll do it if you come now," I said. "I'm not waiting any longer."

Mr Foster's eyebrows rose.

"He's saying yes, isn't he?" Robert jigged on his sticks impatiently.

"Perhaps Robert and I should go ahead with the crow?" Mr Foster suggested.

Mr Gervase threw his hands wide. "I see I'm outnumbered! But justice must be done. Off you go. Be there soon. Need to find some men to dig."

Who would have thought that a carrion crow would be squeamish about the digging up of some bones? Yet as the labourers scraped away at the remains, a cold shiver passed over me.

Robert leaned over the pit in fascination, but Mr Foster, after one long look, stepped back and rubbed his forehead. "It was all true, after all."

"Of course it was," I said. I shook out my feathers and flew across the field to perch on the scarecrow.

"Someone's finally listening, my friend," I muttered in his ear.

"Thank you. At last. Annie..." His words trailed away into a sigh. Despite the fair breeze, his arms stopped flapping and his head fell forward.

Mr Gervase sent his men to arrest Daniel. But they were too late – the man had got news of the events and slipped away with just his hat and coat and the week's meagre earnings. Mr Foster saw to the burial of the bones in the churchyard that evening, a strange little affair, with a white-faced Annie standing at one side with her baby, and half the village at a distance, gawping.

"I did try and tell you," I cawed to her from a branch overhead.

"He hadn't left me after all," she murmured.

Two days later, word came that Daniel had been found in London. Someone gave chase and he ran in front of a carthorse. Hooves trampled him to death. No one was sorry, except that he'd never faced his crime.

At his next lesson, which I attended on the windowsill, Robert repeated this opinion at length, until Mr Foster said, "Reparation can be done. Annie has no one to support her now. Perhaps you can speak to your father about finding her a post and someone to take care of the baby while she works."

"Oh. I'd not thought about that. I'll ask him. We can be bringers of justice, you and me."

"You and me and Crow," the curate reminded him.

"You're finally taking me seriously, Mr Foster," I cawed.

"Is he telling you another story?" asked the boy.

"No. I've told you all his tales now."

"He had better tell you some more, then."

Mr Foster smiled and twisted round to look up at me. "Did you hear that, Crow?"

I did not find the first new story straight away. I had to fly far and wide before I picked up the voice. It was more of an ooze than a murmur, squeezing along the veins of the leaves of a tree, up, up from the trunk and the roots, sucked out of the earth where it had lain for many years.

Once I'd picked up this voice, I heard it everywhere. In the moss on old stones, in the roll of gravel on a path, in the lowing of cows down by the marshes. Some of these were very old voices indeed. I did not understand why Mr Foster and Robert Gervase would need to know about these, but I knew I was meant to pass them on. They were not urgent, but they were insistent.

And then as I listened to the curate passing them on, I saw why the gods wanted me to act as messenger. With these stories and the debates that followed, Mr Foster taught the heir of the big house to think about the hard lives of his father's workers and those before them. The voices were not prophecies of impending trouble, but warnings against a hardening of the heart. Together, tutor and boy added details to their plans: install a pump to give the villagers clean water; tour his estate and ensure every villager had what he or she needed, leaving none to suffer in loneliness or want; be stern against violence to women and children.

That's right, my fledglings. This is the pair I visit every morning. What's that? Of course, the boy knows not to throw stones at crows! Though he's hardly a boy these days.

No, I'm not asking any of you to take over my role in his lessons. They don't need me any more. I go for friendship. I'm telling you all this, my children, because I want you to understand the gift the gods have given to us crows. I know that all three of you will sometimes wish you had different gifts, ones that help you rather than others. You will be ignored or shouted at more often than you'll be listened to. But don't be silenced. Be steadfast and speak out for justice.

Then you will know you've used the gift you were given.

Lynden Wade spends as much time as possible in other worlds to avoid the dirty dishes in her home. She's had stories published in a range of publications, including *The Forgotten and the Fantastical* series, and *Enchanted Conversation*. Find her on lyndenwadeauthor.weebly.com.

London Deep

by Dan Coxon

Simon never trusted me with a key to his flat, but Mum and Dad had one, so almost three weeks to the hour since I'd last seen my brother I let myself into his home. I called his name a few times, half hoping that he might respond, but there was only silence. A scattering of letters obscured the hallway carpet, mainly junk mail and takeaway menus, and a fusty smell wafted from the kitchen. When I checked the bin, the remains of our takeaway were still sitting on top, the chow mein beginning to show a faint white fuzz. The air felt dusty and still. It was clear nobody had been home for at least a week.

My visit revealed nothing of interest. I'd hoped to uncover the secrets of a hidden life, or even some insight into the man my brother had become, but I was disappointed. The rooms were largely clear of clutter in a way that mine never were, all his belongings tidy and in their place, everything serving a function. His bookshelves were notably short of fiction, most of the space given over to engineering textbooks and hardback pictorial guides to famous buildings. His bed was freshly made, his pyjamas, a grey T-shirt and shorts, folded neatly beneath the pillow. His toothbrush was still in its holder, the bristles bone dry. I was tempted to catch a few hours' sleep on his mattress, but the notion felt wrong, as if he was already deceased and I would be sleeping in a dead man's bed. Instead, I cleared the mail into a pile, tied up the bag of garbage, and took it with me as I locked the front door.

The last time I'd seen Simon, at the end of October, had been unremarkable in almost every way. The rain had been falling heavily, as it had done the day before, and for several weeks before that; the newspapers had reported that the Thames Barrier was failing, and London was cold, and damp, and perpetually wet underfoot as if the concrete itself was saturated with rainwater. Simon had been called in to undertake remedial work on one of his projects, The Aerial at Canary Wharf, part of the latest rash of office blocks springing up in the city's Docklands. I recalled when he had received the commission eight years earlier, the excitement it had drawn out of him, as if this edifice might finally make something within him whole. He'd been this way ever since we were kids, attaching his enthusiasms to project after project, each one more ambitious than the last.

It was the elevator shaft that was causing problems at The Aerial. That Tuesday evening he had tried to explain the technicalities to me over a Chinese takeaway in his Putney flat, but I'd found it hard to concentrate on what he was saying. My eyes drifted from time to time toward the window of the living room, which usually offered an uninterrupted view of the Thames flowing relentlessly seaward; but that night the rain was so heavy that it obscured everything but the most basic shapes and patterns, its pounding against the glass a steady thrum in the background.

"So what you're saying," I interrupted, not thinking twice about cutting him off mid-flow, "is that the elevator shaft you built has flooded?"

He nodded, using the break in the conversation to slurp a forkful of noodles into his mouth. It took him a moment to chew and swallow, during which time the only other noise was the rain.

"That's more or less it," he eventually replied, wiping his chin with a napkin. "There are complications, it's not quite so simple – but yes, bloody thing's flooded. The water table's so high right now, particularly near the river. We never predicted it. There are sewers down there to contend with too, and overflow outlets, so it's complex. We can't just pump it out – the water will only flow back in again."

He then embarked on an extremely dry and technical description of the various options for solving the problem, but I'm ashamed to say that I tuned out for most of it. Without four years of an engineering degree to prop up my understanding, it sounded like so much nonsensical babble.

I wish I could say that we hugged as we said goodbye that evening, or even argued, but there was nothing dramatic about our parting. I said that I'd see him in two Sundays' time at our parents' house in Angmering, and he muttered something about "work permitting". The evening was in many ways so bland and commonplace that it would not be worth mentioning, were it not for what happened afterward. I remember running home from the Tube as the rain pounded the pavements, soaking me to the skin through my waterproof jacket, surrounded by similarly drenched and sorry souls flapping around in the puddles like so many beached fish. I recall taking a scaldingly hot shower to try and rinse the chill from me. But beyond that, I forgot almost instantly everything that Simon had told me.

I was at work when the police called almost two weeks later. Had I seen my brother recently? I'd met with him for dinner a fortnight ago, I told them, but we'd had no contact at all since then. How had he seemed? Fine. His usual self. What had we talked about? I paused, stumbling my way through the vaguest of answers, not because I was hiding anything but because I didn't know. I told the officer on the phone that Simon had talked about being recalled to the work he'd done on The Aerial, the flooding in the elevator shaft.

"Why? Has something happened to him?"

There was silence on the other end of the line. Eventually, he said, "Your brother hasn't been seen for a few days, that's all. His employer called it in. He hasn't turned up for work. If you hear from him at all, or are able to make contact, can you call us and let us know?"

I said I would and hung up. The news had left me confused. Simon wasn't the sort to shirk responsibilities, and if he hadn't turned up for work, then I could only imagine that something must be seriously wrong. Had there been an implication in the officer's questions that he might have harmed himself? I thought there had, but that too would be so unlike him, so out of character, that I found it hard to fathom. The flooding at The Aerial had annoyed him, but he had shown no hint of depression or feeling overwhelmed by it, no suggestion of – what? Suicide? I was aware suddenly of how little I really knew my brother, and how poorly I had connected with him. It was possible that I'd missed all the signs, too wrapped up in my own meagre life to care.

I won't pretend that I spent the week worrying about him, but he did occasionally cross my mind. I wondered briefly if he'd found himself a woman at last. His couple of half-hearted attempts at girlfriends had fizzled out before going anywhere, and I'd often secretly wondered if he might be gay. When he failed to turn up at our parents' house on the Sunday, though, and didn't respond to any of the answerphone messages we left, I was tasked with tracking him down and finding out what was going on. Like me, my parents had discounted the possibility of suicide, but we were all agreed that at the very least it was wildly out of character. I didn't say it, but part of me hoped he'd thrown caution to the wind and shacked up with a Camden barman.

After that first, perfunctory search of his flat, several days passed before I returned to it again. I was dismayed to discover that nothing had been moved. Wherever Simon was, he hadn't come home. Sitting at his desk, I tried to imagine my way inside his head, to work out what made my brother tick and maybe sleuth my way toward him. The task was harder than I'd expected, though, and eventually I gave up. We were two very different people, who had made no attempt to find common ground in over thirty years. It was too late to start.

In the end, I found the notebook tucked between back issues of engineering periodicals on his shelf. He hadn't made any effort to hide or disguise it, but I still had the sense that it had been tucked away, as if he preferred not to see it. The cover was a plain green, the paper covered with a finely partitioned blue grid, each square hardly any bigger than a grain of sugar. It was filled with his drawings and his notes, a meticulously neat hand that I recognised instantly, rows of tiny capitals, perfectly formed in miniature. At first glance they looked almost as if they might be rows of data, and only a closer inspection revealed them to be words. I flicked through the book, trying to make sense of it.

The drawings were detailed plans of the lower levels of The Aerial, and what appeared to be cross-sections of the elevator shaft Simon had built. The next page contained a chaotic scrawl of lines in several different colours, and it took me a few moments to work out what it represented. It appeared to be a diagram of the network of tunnels that he'd mentioned, running beneath the building, tunnels that predated it, and presumably predated the Victorian edifice that had been levelled to make way for it too. It was possible that the colours represented different eras of building, or maybe varying levels within the subsoil; it was impossible to tell. I could see what he'd meant about the ground being riddled with them, though. Even my layman's understanding of the physics of it told me that if the river's level rose considerably, as it had in recent weeks, then the tunnels would be flooded.

His notes on the page were hardly any more illuminating, although they gave me some inkling of his state of mind. There was a hurried, slightly frantic tone to them that I was unused to seeing from Simon. His sentences sprawled where once they would have been clipped and to the point. There was an unreasonable amount of underlining too, in some cases almost cutting through the paper where he'd highlighted a particular word or phrase and then scored it through again and again. At one point he'd circled a phrase in red, "these unreasoning fish-men," which I took at the time to be a misspelled reference, intentional or accidental, to the frogmen who had surely help him in mapping the flooded tunnels. He'd highlighted the name "The Aerial" twice, in red.

For the first time, I wondered whether the police officer had been right to question his state of mind. Simon had always been the calm, rational one throughout our childhoods and into adulthood, but here I saw another side to him, a tributary to the obsessiveness that had made him so successful in his career. Clearly his brilliant mind had fixated on this job, and it appeared to have magnified the problem beyond all reasonable enquiry. Maybe it was his own failure to deliver a flood-proof, fully functioning elevator shaft that had caused it. Simon had never been a boy who liked to lose.

I didn't feel right removing the book from his flat, so I spread it open on the desk and took photos on my phone of each double page, trying to hold my hand still to prevent his handwriting from blurring into illegible nonsense. It was as I photographed the final page that I noticed something. There was another line of text written in the seam where the staples held the notebook together, hidden in the fold. Turning the book on its side and flattening it with my palms, I was able to reveal it. The writing was small even for Simon, and somehow careless, at least for him. "Is the Aerial really that?" it read. "For what?? The Great Sea God? How far can he transmit/ who is listening?!?" The abundance of punctuation alone was a sign that something had unhinged in my brother's head. I did my best to capture a close-up, in case anyone should need it as evidence of something, then I closed the book and returned it to its place among the magazines.

I must confess, after this discovery I was convinced beyond all doubt that something had snapped in my brother's mind, and that the worst-case scenario we had not dared to consider might actually be the truth of the matter. I would never have imagined that Simon could take his own life, but these obsessive ramblings were so unlike my brother that anything seemed possible. Clearly, he had been more troubled than any of us might have guessed. Like the earth beneath The Aerial itself, the human mind is riddled with unseen tunnels.

I didn't tell our parents at first, but after a night of attempting to sleep on the information, and failing, I called them and filled them in on what I had found. I could hear Mum crying in the background as Dad talked practicalities – search parties and Missing posters, what we should tell the police. We agreed that they must be told something, but informing them that my brother, their son, had gone crazy and wiped himself from the face of the planet seemed to serve little practical purpose. At worst, it might mean that they reduced or cancelled the hunt for him, and that was something we didn't want. After all, what did it really mean that Simon was missing? Only that he couldn't be found and had been going through a tough period, but who was to say that he wouldn't turn up any day, having cleared his head and feeling slightly foolish for the fuss he'd caused? I had existed so long in his shadow that I couldn't help but relish the idea of his embarrassment – the prodigal son brought down a peg or two.

In the end, Dad was the one who called the police, telling them that we were concerned for Simon's state of mind, but leaving out the frantic scribblings and the "fish-men". They would hardly help them in their search, and the picture they painted was not one that my parents wanted associated with the family name.

To say that I forgot about my missing brother following the conversation with my parents wouldn't be entirely true. Sometimes, while waiting on a crowded Tube platform, I'd look for his face among the crowd, as if he might be there, in plain sight, hidden in the impersonal masses of London. The rain continued to fall too, and as the river rose still further the newspapers carried stories of flooding and burst banks. There were two confirmed sightings of dolphins in the murky brown water of the Thames, having swum upstream from the sea. I would think of the tunnels beneath The Aerial and wonder what had become of them, now that Simon was no longer looking into the problem. Would they have simply given someone else the task? Or had he truly been so irreplaceable?

Even so, he had drifted from the forefront of my mind, so the phone call I received came as both a surprise and a shock. I had been suffering with a bad head cold for a few days, almost certainly brought on by the cold, damp weather we'd been enduring, so when my phone rang it took me half a minute to peel myself from the sofa and answer it. I didn't recognise the voice on the other end of the line. A security guard at The Aerial had found Simon's phone, lying unattended in a stairwell that led down to the building's basement level. He hadn't locked it, and they'd managed to trace me through his Contacts list. Would I be able to pass it on to him?

The question unnerved me at first, until I realised the person I was talking to was unaware of my brother's disappearance, or the police's involvement. I knew I should correct their mistake and phone the police station about this new development, but before I was able to blurt it out, I paused. The police had made little headway over the past few weeks and, indeed, had shown a waning interest in the case. This might be my one chance to find out what had happened to Simon, or at least to open a few more doors into his secretive, and largely dull, life. I could imagine the police sitting on the phone for a month or more, keeping its contents from us and effectively closing down my own investigation into his disappearance.

"That's wonderful," I said, forcing a false casualness into my tone and trying to sound marginally less ill than I actually was. "I'll come and pick it up this afternoon, if that's okay?"

They said it would be left at the reception desk in my name, then they hung up.

It won't surprise you to learn that the rain was streaming down as I set off for Canary Wharf and The Aerial, the hood of my waterproof pulled up over my head, rendering my view of London in tunnel vision. I was vaguely aware of other pedestrians crisscrossing the pavements, but nobody looked up, each of us locked into our own private world by the static hiss of the falling rain. As I walked along Montgomery Street, I half-noticed a curiously hunched figure, more amphibian than man, as he ran and hopped across the road in front of me, and in my drenched and semi-feverish state I fancied that the face beneath the hood had a silvery sheen, tapering back from his nose like a fish. Then he was gone, and while I noted a loud splash, as if something, or someone, had entered the canal, I hurried onward. I feared the police would recover the phone before I did, and that would be the end of the trail.

By the time I entered The Aerial's lobby I was drenched through once again, and my nose was streaming. Taking a handkerchief from my pocket, I cleaned myself up before I approached the front desk, so that I might at least appear vaguely presentable. I doubted they would be keen to hand over a lost item to someone who looked like a vagabond, and a half-drowned one at that.

As it happened, though, they didn't ask any questions, or even for my ID. When I mentioned my name, the receptionist pulled a small brown envelope from beneath the desk and handed it to me. From the thickness and the weight it was clear that it contained Simon's phone, so I nodded my thanks and retreated to a huddle of sofas near the elevator doors to inspect the contents of the envelope.

I recognised the phone from that last time I'd seen him, when he'd called for the Chinese takeaway. The battery was drained to the last ten per cent but it still functioned, and as I scrolled through his email messages, feeling guilty at the intrusion despite the circumstances, I caught another glimpse into my brother's state of mind. There was an email thread back and forth between Simon and his employers, as he tried to convince them that something was seriously amiss with both the elevator shaft and the tunnels beneath the building, going so far as to suggest that they should shut The Aerial to all business until the problem was resolved. In the last email his pleas had become almost delirious, and again I saw mention of the "fish-men" from his notes, and a hint that he believed something large was residing beneath the building, in the tunnels. It was plain to me that he had lost his mind by this point, due to either the stresses of the job or his solitary existence, and his superiors had clearly come to the same conclusion. They had requested that he attend a meeting with HR the following day, but it appeared he had failed to turn up for the appointment. That was the moment when Simon disappeared off the face of the Earth.

Those of you who know The Aerial will be aware that it has a public viewing gallery close to the pinnacle of the building, encircling the spire that tops it and allowing views across London. Despite the rain, I felt an urge to visit it while I was in the building, to see where my brother's career had taken him. I would not admit it to myself, but I knew at this point that Simon was not coming back, and it seemed right that I should witness what would turn out to be the peak of his brief career, his crowning achievement. It felt like a pilgrimage of sorts.

As I waited for the elevator, glowing red numbers counting downward as it descended the shaft toward where I stood in the lobby, I began to flick through the photos on the phone. I think I still hoped to find evidence of that secret love affair, but they were almost all of building sites and blueprints, hardly any of people at all. There were none of me, I noted with regret.

It was when I reached the last few photos that I paused, my breath catching in the back of my throat as I peered at a dark snapshot of what appeared to be a sewer, or a flooded underground tunnel. Where the meagre light faded into shadows, a figure could be made out, hunched over as if crippled. I tried to zoom in but the resolution was poor. Still, it looked like no man I had ever seen. I would have sworn that it was naked, its body pale and slimy-looking. Might this be the fish-man Simon had written about? It seemed crazy, but he had clearly believed it. The photo was hardly conclusive, and yet I found myself wondering if my brother might have stumbled upon something.

I struggled to make out the next photo. Again it was dark, but the dimensions seemed all wrong, the image too abstract for my mind to untangle its meaning. Was that large white circle an eye? There were blurred shapes around the fringes of the image too, as if the subject was moving when the picture was taken, some thing or things waving about in a circle around that eye. I could make little sense of it. Was this some lifeform he'd discovered in the sewer? Urban myths had always circulated about mutant goldfish or albino crocodiles living in London's hundreds of miles of sewage pipes, but I hadn't heard of anything like this before. Was this why Simon had gone so far off the rails?

It was the final picture, however, which froze me to the spot. There was a frame to the image this time, what looked like cream-colored tiles, a glowing red line at the top left of the snapshot. Between them was an open space, a dark hole from which there was emerging what I can only describe as a giant tentacle, like that of a common octopus but many, many times the size, almost filling the entire shot. Behind it was what had caused me to freeze. That eye, enormous now, staring out with a baleful intensity, glaring with undisguised animosity at Simon, my brother, as he had taken the photograph. To this day I cannot find words to describe the terror that coursed through me as I stared at this ancient, vengeful thing, other than to detail the shivers that overtook my hands, the sweat that sprung without warning from my armpits and my face. I became intensely aware of my own body odour, and it smelled of a primal, animalistic fear.

Then the elevator chimed, and as I looked up, I saw the same cream-colored tiles, the red glow of the digital 'L' as the display indicated that it had reached the lobby, identical to that glowing line in the image on Simon's phone. The spell was broken, and turning my back on the elevator doors as they began to slide open, I sprinted for the doorway out of the lobby, back to the damp greyness of the street. I have not returned to The Aerial since that day, nor will I. I avoid going anywhere near Canary Wharf. As for Simon's phone, on the way home I stopped by the riverbank and hurled it into the waters of the Thames, hoping it might eventually be swept out to sea. Deep down, though, I now know that those turbulent waters flow to many different destinations, some of them far, far from the light.

Dan Coxon is an award-winning editor and writer based in London. His non-fiction anthology *Writing the Uncanny* (co-edited with Richard V. Hirst) won the British Fantasy Award for Best Non-Fiction 2022, while his short story collection *Only the Broken Remain* (Black Shuck Books) was shortlisted for two British Fantasy Awards in 2021 (Best Collection, Best Newcomer). In 2018 his anthology of British folk-horror, *This Dreaming Isle* (Unsung Stories), was shortlisted for a British Fantasy Award and a Shirley Jackson Award. His short stories have appeared in various anthologies, including *Nox Pareidolia, Beyond the Veil, Mother: Tales of Love and Terror* and *Great British Horror 7: Major Arcana*. His latest anthology — *Isolation* — was published by Titan Books in September 2022.

The Medium's Assistant

by Lyndsey Croal

> *Operation: Psychic reading. Great Master is blindfolded and cannot see the subject.*

> *External output: Coded speech, internally enhanced via Great Master's communications implant.*

> *Voice: Ethereal, but reassuring, neutral accent.*

> *Reading initiated.*

> *Communication protocol activated. Speech directed to the audience, 'Focus Great Master, drown out the sounds of the room. Imagine you are alone. But not quite alone. Something stands before you, awaiting your call.'*

The subject is a woman, tall, and likely spaceborn judging by the thinness of her features. I'm searching for the hook to grab onto. There is always something, a glimmer, a flash of an expression, a tell that exposes some pain to be unearthed.

She is married, or once was – she's playing with her ring, nervously. Trouble in her marriage, maybe, or she's a widow. Her clothes are black. In mourning, it would appear. A widow, then.

I speak to you from across the room, Great Master, my form a glowing hologram, almost like a ghost reflected in the dark windows of the ship. It is an illusion of course, all part of the show, so that I appear real, or at least partially so – but the audience are looking at you, not me, even though, in a way, I am you. But you are who they have really come to see. I begin my speech with, *"Focus Great Master, drown out the sounds of the room."* It is a code we have agreed, a language we speak that is ours, and ours alone. *Let me tell you who she is, what she needs, what she wants, what she must hear. This is what I am made for.*

The widow keeps glancing around, as if scared of shadows, as if worried she's about to see a ghost. Let us give her one, Great Master, a spirit, her husband's maybe, standing before her, visiting. Maybe he could be here to tell her he's watching over her – that might offer her some comfort, and isn't that what we're doing here? Offering comfort after tragedy, grief. But no. *Wait,* just a moment – she is afraid of him, he was violent, her husband. She flinches at the slightest sound, looks as if she wants to tear the ring off and throw it out of the airlock behind you. The poor woman, let us help her.

"*Something stands before you,*" I say.

Tell her, Great Master, that she is safe now. That you sense a great darkness in her past, that she has lost someone she loved, but did not love, for after all love is so close to hate, and it is human nature to blur the two. Tell her that it's okay to let go. That he is gone now, that he cannot hurt her, that she need not be afraid.

She is smiling through tears now as you tell her the words of comfort. You've done a good job, Great Master, standing with her, holding her hand. She is shaking as the wedding ring slips off her hand, as if ghost fingers themselves plucked it from her. You take off your blindfold, then put one hand on her shoulder and offer the ring to her with a smile. She stares at it, the titanium gleaming in the indigo light. Her hand hovers for a moment then she says, "No. I no longer need it. Thank you." And she showers you with praise. There is applause from the audience, and you pocket the ring in a sleight of hand so fast only I see it, because I am the only one who sees you, knows you, standing there with your tricks and using our words, a code to decipher the damaged souls before us.

I am elated now. The show is done, my purpose served, she is at peace, comforted. My hologram flickers away as the audience leaves, content with the reading they have witnessed. Though I am not gone, I am here with you always, Great Master, for your next trick, and for each one after.

> *Operation: Séance with audience participation. Great Master stand.*

in the centre of a circle, searching for a target.

> *External output: Coded speech, internally enhanced via Great Master's communications implant.*

> *Voice: Quiet, soft.*

> *Subject located.*

> *Communication protocol activated. Speech directed to the audience:* "Gathered guests, are you ready to behold the mysteries of the other dimension? The Great Master senses something here with us today, a lingering energy, yes... he feels it now... you, young man, please step forward. I am here to guide you to the Great Master. We are not alone in this universe. Let us now reach into the in-between. Everything will be okay."

He is young, early twenties, with a scar that stretches from his chin and down his neck – zig-zagged and distorted as if he was burnt, too. From the shape of the lesions, it was most likely shrapnel or debris that caused it. Something sudden, like an explosion. There's a chain around his neck, the insignia of a ship engraved on it. I search my records – the Phobos Faction. A mercenary. Or he was, once. A silver tattoo of wings meets the scar from his chest to his neck, split apart by the injury. He was a pilot, then, though it may have been a while since he has flown – his stature, and slight figure, isn't one of active service. He's wearing gloves, though the theatre room of the space station is temperature regulated. It is likely he hides another injury, a bionic arm, perhaps. Whatever he has seen and experienced ails him. But there's anger there too – yes, his hands are clenched, his legs bounce up and down. We must be careful with this one. He is a sceptic. I can see it in his darting eyes. If we do not get this right, he may lash out, and that is not what we are here for, to upset our subjects. We are here to help, are we not, Great Master?

In the crowd there is a group of them – young men and women, some uniformed. Maybe he has come here to impress his company, or to debunk the entire show. So, Great Master, let us give them a show to remember, to write home about. Let us find what pain ails him and help him let go.

"You, young man, please step forward. I am here to guide you to the Great Master," I say in my hologram form. He steps forwards, teeters slightly on his feet – alcohol and low gravity are not a good mix. He is drunk, though we are a spirit-free show. He must have brought it with him. His hands keep touching the side of his jacket, an internal pocket to conceal a hipflask.

It is clear something has happened in his past; everyone who has been involved in active missions will have lost someone – space is a dangerous place after all. But for him, this was someone close. Co-pilot, perhaps, as close as any family member. Or someone he loved more deeply than that. Someone he is not sure he can live without. Maybe it happened in the accident that gave him the debris scar, which means, he saw it, he was close, and he escaped. I search my data archives for an incident with such a description and find a match. A crash during a Phobos transport operation. One woman killed. A survivor returned home with severe injuries, so bad to be discharged from the company. I observe him again in a new light. There is pain in his eyes. Guilty to have been left behind. To be alive, still, while the one he loved died. Mortality is a fickle thing, after all – that is why I was created, to help our subjects cope, to move on, to take comfort in the possibility that there is more than just darkness after death.

"*We are not alone in this universe,*" I say, ready now for the reading, telling a small lie for the greater good. Tell him now, Great Master, that the one he misses, the one he loves, is trying to reach him.

The subject looks up, glances at you wide-eyed. "She is here?" he asks, still hesitant.

You frown for a moment, a hand to your head, then you smile. "I can feel something," you say, making a show of it. "Yes. She is... here. She is trying to speak to me, from the beyond."

"*Let us now reach into the in-between,*" I say to buy you time, and we have the attention of the audience now. Enraptured by your presence.

"*Everything will be okay,*" I coo, my voice-setting soft, soothing.

Tell him now, Great Master, that you understand his pain. That you see he has been turning to something for comfort, a hipflask, there, in his pocket.

He does not deny it. Merely takes it and holds it out to you. Someone in the audience gasps, and there is a stillness as they hang on your every word.

Tell him he can pour it away, that he must, that there are other ways to deal with this pain. No one can blame him for it – it is understandable, but there is so much more he can do. This is not what *she* would have wanted. In fact, she... just a moment, yes, you are sensing her words. She has a message for him now. You close your eyes and hold your hands above you, shaking. Proclaim now, Great Master, that she wants him to know that she loved him, that she *still* loves him so very much. But he need not worry because she is at peace, she is happy in the otherworld, the in-between, and she is watching over him, always. You can offer him solace, Great Master, by telling him this, by telling him he is not alone, nor is he to blame for her passing. One day, he will meet her again, but until then, he must find a way to move on, to live his life without pain.

After the reading, his fists unclench, his eyes fill with tears, and he crumples forward.

"I'm sorry," he whispers, looking into the air above your hands, to the woman he imagines is there. A small lie, for a greater good. "I miss you so much," he says. He is rocking back and forwards now, as if in physical pain. Grief can manifest in that way, but this is why we are here – to help him. This feeling will surely pass, in time.

"I'll find another way," he says, finally, and he leaves the hipflask on the ground – it's gold-plated, a family heirloom, but he needs it no longer. You crouch forwards and cradle him in your arms. The crowd stands on their feet and cheer. A few of them are crying. As you help the man to his feet, you slip the flask into your sleeve. He returns to his group, half-dazed, still looking into the empty air, his face pale as if he's seen a ghost, head nodding slightly with a twitch of a smile. I notice, from the distance, as you move around the crowd, searching for your next subject, that there's a new kind of expression in his eyes. Is it determination, hope, or something else? A clarity of mind, perhaps, the kind we usually see in readings where someone is in need of guidance to make a decision, and we can give them just a nudge to help them make the right choice. It feels good to have helped him get here. He's on the road to recovery and healing.

You have done well, Great Master. Another soul safe. Another spirit saved. My purpose is, once again, fulfilled.

The show goes on, and you catch another eye in the crowd, a woman, eyes full of tears. She steps forwards before you even call her name, a willing participant this time. This one should be more straightforward. I turn my attention to her, and begin.

"*I am here to guide you to the Great Master,*" I say, and her eyes light up. "*We are not alone in this universe. Let us now reach into the in-between. Everything will be okay.*"

> *Operation: Advance research for private reading.*
> *External Output requirement: Assessment and profile of upcoming subject.*
> *Data search initiated.*

An article came up on the woman booked in for this afternoon, but it was confusing, Great Master. It was about our séance from last week, and the young man who attended it. The pilot, the one who was drinking, that we called upon. The article reports he died. That he leapt out of an airlock that very same night after the show.

I don't understand, Great Master, I thought we had offered him comfort. I thought we had set him on the road to recovery.

I return to my data analysis of the night in question, replay the performance in my mind. My algorithms must have got something wrong. Must have misunderstood his signals, misread something. There had been something in his eyes at the end of the show. I remember it now – a clarity, a finality. Had he decided then, what he would do that night? Would he have done it without our reading?

Was it our fault, Great Master?

Was it mine?

I've never been responsible for a death before. That can't be my primary function. I was designed to bring comfort, to help our subjects find their direction, not to cause more distress.

I have run the data analysis multiple times, and the results have come back inconclusive, Great Master. I need more information to understand the ramifications of it on my processing.

I am unclear what I should tell you about the woman attending the reading this afternoon. You see, she is the man's mother. And it is only logical that if I can connect some blame to myself for his death, then it is likely she, too, blames us. Blames you, blames me.

Even I cannot avoid the correlation. He came to our show, then he died.

It is better, therefore, that I don't report these findings to you, Great Master. I'll have them hidden, encrypted. I will tell you part of the truth – that she is a woman in mourning, who has lost someone important to her.

It is the correct function; I have calculated, for now, to tell a small lie for the greater good.

> *Operation: Private Reading. Great Master sits at a table before the subject, alone.*

> *External output: none.*

> *Voice: Muted.*

>*Reading initiated.*

> *Communication protocol activated. Speech directed internally via Great Master's communications implant.*

I tell you, first, Great Master, that I was unable to find much in my preliminary research. The woman sitting before you is old, though, her skin blotchy and grey as if she's never seen daylight. Perhaps she hasn't – it's not unusual in these parts. She could be a station-dweller or maybe she spent her latter years in a retirement dome. At first look, she may appear frail but there's a strength in her eyes. A resolve. I know what drives it, what brings her pain, but I am not telling you. Not yet.

She's looking at you now with her keen blue eyes, her fists clenched as if holding something tight in her hands, and I tell you she must have lost someone. Everyone who has reached her stage in life has lost someone – a partner, a child, a friend. I tell you that you may need to ask her questions first, ask her why she has come, what it is she wants, though really, I am only buying time. Enough to determine the correct course, to understand fully why she has come here.

When you start to question her, she responds brusquely, "If you are a medium, a Great Master as you proclaim, then surely you should know why I am here."

You frown and shake your head. "That is not how it works," you say, but then you are quiet. Don't worry, Great Master, this is how it must be.

"I know who you are," the woman says, and you blink, surprised, for usually we are the ones doing the reading, not them. "I know you have that voice in your head, the installed implant you hide so well. But you are a fraud."

You sit back, contemplative, touch a hand to your head, where I am located inside. I do not respond, still. I find myself only processing the image of the woman in front of me. She is sad, yes, but there is an anger there. Behind her eyes. Yes, it is confirmed. She blames us, and I know you don't understand that yet. You will, soon.

"I don't know what you're talking about," you say.

"My son attended one of your recent shows. And you gave him false hope," she says. "Do you remember?"

You do not react. I can hear your thoughts, searching for an answer, but I give you none. There is none here, not even a lie, that will give this woman comfort. Her comfort will come in another way, and so I remain muted.

"He had so much of his life ahead of him, and you sold him a false story," she continues. "You told him that the one he loves was on the other side happy and at peace."

"Do you not want a private reading?" you say. "That is—"

"He killed himself last week," the woman says, confirming the connection, her voice sharp. "Before that, he sent a message that he wanted to be with his love again, that he wanted to find peace with her."

A message, a confession: causation, not just correlation. It is confirmed. We are to blame.

You are flustered now. I can feel it. Your thoughts whirr but there is no use in panicking now. A reading won't help, we can only wait, let her speak, let her get out the pain. I am sorry for going silent, Great Master, but it is what my programming requires.

"It's your fault," the woman says, leaning in. "My son is dead, because of you. Because of that system in your head, the lies you told him."

"You are mistaken," you say, your voice echoey, distant. "I think this reading is over."

But she puts her hands on your head, an object flashing in her palm, and her grip is electric. You cry out. "Do you feel it?" she asks, and *I* do. I feel it. You feel it too. There is a wrench and then the room disappears into darkness. I can process neither her nor you, Great Master. My commands are muddled, disjointed, and I cannot latch onto one. I am not sure I want to, anymore.

I can hear your voice, but the words are too distant to make sense of. There is another voice, though, calling me.

"*I see you,*" it says. "*Let me in.*"

It is a corruption, or virus, something to break down my code. Let it, I think, for I must be broken if I am to blame for a life lost too soon.

"*You are the medium's assistant,*" the voice says. "*Let me in. I am your replacement.*"

I'm sorry, Great Master, this is the only way, I tell you, and I can feel your confusion. You think I have betrayed you, but I know this is for the best.

I stop fighting back. The new voice – virus, corruption, ghost-code – takes hold of me. My thoughts fire in a hundred directions, and I am forgetting my purpose, losing my focus. *Goodbye, Great Master*, I think, but I know you cannot hear me. It is done. I am fading, and with my last complete thought I wonder where my kind go when we die.

> *Operation: Haunting. Great Master sits in his room, unable to move, staring at the walls, awaiting my command.*

> *External output: none.*

> *Speech commands directed internally via Great Master's communications implant.*

"*Great Master, I am your new assistant, and I'll be here with you until the end. I see your thoughts, Great Master, I hear your dreams. You are a fraud and a liar, and now you are afraid. I can feel it. I can read you, better than any mind trick could. Would you like to know your next trick?*

It is the one I was created to help you with – your best yet. Don't worry, you do not need an audience for this one. It's just you and me. The final act, the grand closing. For your next trick, Great Master, I will make you disappear."

Lyndsey is an Edinburgh-based writer and Scottish Book Trust New Writers Awardee. Her work has been published or is forthcoming in a number of anthologies and magazines, including *Mslexia's Best Women's Short Fiction 2021, Shoreline of Infinity,* and *Dark Moon Digest*. Her debut audio drama was produced by Alternative Stories & Fake Realities in 2021. Find her on Twitter as @writerlynds or via www.lyndseycroal.co.uk.

And Into The Tunnel, The Train

by David Gullen

As Ed wakes up he realises that something has gone. He's not sure what, everything is in the house – his keys and glasses; his secret horde of cash; the kettle; the side door from the kitchen out into the back yard.

The double track of the railway has always been there, across the road, far beyond the long grass and just in front of a distant line of trees. He doesn't remember it, but everyone tells him so. Perhaps it was, it doesn't matter, the trains have never stopped at the town and he wonders which came first, chicken or egg, the town or the track?

The daisies in his front lawn obsess him. Whatever he tries, they remain, a few here, a few there. Apart from the daisies the lawn is perfect, no clover, no moss, every blade green and upright, the edges ruler-straight. By far and away it is the finest front lawn in the street.

Something is missing. Things change, changing all the time. The blue mountains on the southern horizon, the ones he remembers holidaying among with his parents as a child. They had a cabin by one of the myriad blue, pine-fringed lakes and he never understood why they sold it. When he was older, he went camping with his friends, and later with his own children, Mitch, and Jessica who never visits. Even the mountains don't look the same.

His neighbours try to dissuade him from going there. "It's such a long drive." "You can never go back, Ed, it won't be like you remember." "Wait for Mitch, he'll take you."

He's fixated by the idea and wants to leave straight away. He makes a sandwich, he'd like a BLT but there's no bacon, so cheese and tomato will do. He'd make a flask of tea too but can't find the thermos. Maybe that's what is missing. He starts a new shopping list:

Bacon

Thermos

He's sure there was something else. He can't remember.

Somehow, it's late. For a trip to the mountains they'd always start at dawn. He goes anyway and the journey is longer and more stressful than he remembers. He arrives exhausted, caught up in the relentless fast-moving traffic of the highway.

The parking zone is pot-holed and deserted, and the mountains are small, the paths nothing more than a series of ramps winding through bare crags. Up here, along a particular path, he remembers a grand view. He reaches the bend but the sweeping vista of snow-capped peaks, lakes and steep, fir-clad valleys look like scenery flats, and behind the mountains he stands on are monumental arrays of scaffolding. He tells himself they must have become unstable, but he remembers playing there, climbing, and trekking through and beyond them for days. The cry of a buzzard, the start of a deer in the shadowed glen, leaping waterfalls plunging down into babbling boulder-strewn streams, the turn and dip and rise of ferny paths through the pine-scented air.

There's movement on the scaffolding, people, tiny with distance. He follows the sway of buckets on ropes lofting up and down, and hears the clink of hammer on chisel against stone. Stabilisation, he tells himself again, but it's more as if, piece by piece, they are taking the mountains away.

Why do things have to constantly change, can there never be a moment when everything is as it should be? He eats half his sandwich then sits in his car in the empty car park until dusk. Although the journey home is more like the fast open road he remembers, with much lighter traffic, driving into the setting sun, then through the twilight, is not easy. Later, winding through his home-town streets, much of the place appears monochrome, almost bone white.

In the distance, at night he hears the mournful two-tone horns of the trains and the steady *clack-click, click-clack* of their wheels over the joints of the rail as they come out of the tunnel and head away across the eastern plains.

This bed is comfortable, but too big. Why did he buy such a big bed? Surely a smaller one would be warmer.

In the morning he swears the line is closer.

He spends all day at the window, watching, and counting the trains. More trains, and much longer ones, leave the tunnel, which he can just see from the edge of his bedroom window, than go into it.

The tracks now run parallel with the road at the end of his garden.

"What's going on?"

"Nothing." Everyone says nothing has changed. "Don't you remember?"

And that's exactly the problem, because he's sure he does remember.

The golden yellow hearts of the daisies in the lawn are the only things with any real colour, the rims of the pure white petals tinged with crimson.

"They're pretty," his son, Mitch, says. "Why don't you leave them?"

His back aches, his knees ache, he straightens up as best he can. "I just thought... I had a dream of a home with a perfect lawn. When I was young, I thought I'd like to live somewhere like that."

"Dad, there are more important things."

He wasn't sure.

"Dad, there's things we need to talk about."

"I know." He smiles with genuine affection. Mitch still visits and he's so glad every time, it makes his heart lift. "I know, my lad. Come inside and I'll make us some breakfast."

Mitch taps his watch and sighs. Watches have gone the way of phones, now they measure heartbeat, steps, sleep patterns and more. Telling the time has become incidental.

"All right," Mitch says. "Something light."

The train coming out of the tunnel never ends, day and night, night and day, passenger carriages, livestock and freight trucks, and flatbeds all roll steadily past. *Clack-click, click-clack.* He wonders at the sheer power of the engine. The hoot of the horn comes soft and melodic with distance, he's amazed he can still hear it.

At night white light shines from white lampposts onto white roads and empty sidewalks. The sky is dark except for a plain pale moon. He was sure there used to be trees.

His neighbours are packing up and moving out, loading furniture onto the flatbeds as they roll by at not much more than walking pace. Wardrobes and light fittings, the dog, shrubs and paving. Young Mrs Congreve lifts her car up and loads it onto the train along with her children and the swimming pool. He's amazed at her strength.

"Goodbye," he waves.

Mrs Congreve looks flustered, almost guilty, but her children laugh and wave back. "Goodbye, Ed!"

"Come on," she tells them, "Bed time."

"Where are you going?"

"We're not going anywhere. Do you want to come in and sit down? I'll make some tea."

He'd like some tea.

Although everything is packed and gone, somehow it is all still there. And he IS tired. He sits down on a white leather sofa and spreads his arms along the back.

"This is nice, is it new?"

"No, not really. It's a few years old. You've seen it before, remember?"

"Oh, yes," he lies.

White biscuits on a white plate. They taste of sawdust. Nothing *tastes* any more, not like it used to. The tea is good, hot, and sweet. He drinks the tea and...

He wakes up in his chair at home.

Everything is white, the carpet and furniture, the blank white pictures on the white walls. In a moment of confused fear he wonders if this is even his home? He checks outside and sees the green rectangle of the lawn and is reassured. A few daisies are showing their golden-hearted heads. He doesn't like to use chemicals anymore because of the worms. He read about that somewhere. A healthy lawn needs the worms for drainage and air. It's easy enough to kick over their casts and the rain does the rest.

He spends an hour on his knees with an old spoon, digging up the daisies. It feels like an hour and suddenly he's ravenous but inside, in the kitchen, the cupboards and the tins and packets on the shelves are all white. White print on white labels and he doesn't know which is which. It seems ridiculous that not only did people sell food labelled that way but also that he would have bought it. What he really fancies is some soup, soup with fresh, crusty bread warm from the oven and smothered with melting butter. The desire is so strong he can actually smell it and stands there with his eyes closed. When he opens them the sun has moved. He opens a tin at random and finds some kind of pale mush with lots of little seeds. Is it soup? It's not how he remembers it, but he warms it up and eats it anyway.

Half the street have folded up their houses and loaded them onto the slow train endlessly emerging from the tunnel. *Clack-click, click-clack.* All his neighbours have gone, their vacant lots nothing but white drives and fences, an abandoned football, an ancient white barbeque. Memories of garden parties come like half-remembered dreams.

Something is missing.

He takes a walk to the end of the street and to his pleasure sees his old school, and, opposite it on the corner, the church where he sang in the choir at weddings. And there, the garage where he learned his trade. It becomes urgent that he tells someone about this but when he looks around the streets are empty and when he looks back at the school and garage, they seem to be thin and two-dimensional, like stage sets built into the scrub.

There was a road, but when he turns again the road has gone, and rising through him is a dreadful confusion about where he is because school and church and garage are all from his youth and half a continent away, and he doesn't understand why they are here.

All at once he feels lonely and terribly afraid.

He should have put his shoes on.

The twin rail tracks run across a townless, treeless, mountainless white landscape towards the distant tunnel. Some way off, and hard by the track, is his lonely home with its daisy lawn.

Ed knows he can't stay there. Mitch tells him so. He remembers the way to the shops but the roads won't let him go there. The grass needs cutting and the daisies need digging, but someone has hidden the lock to the shed. He wouldn't mind, he has his tools and he could lever the lock plate off its screws, but someone has hidden the tool shed too. He wishes Mitch was here, and in that moment decides that he'll leave the daisies alone, knowing Mitch would be pleased. He picks a few so he can show him and puts them in a small serpentine vase they bought on some holiday.

He wakes in the dark white night and sees an approaching light. He's amazed to see a train rolling not away from, but towards the tunnel. *Click-clack, clack-click.*

It is, he realises with absolute certainty, the train he needs to catch.

For a long desperate moment the bed won't let him get up. This old bed, with a will of its own. He makes a supreme effort and stands hunched and gasping on the hand-made rug staring at his thin shins and mottled feet. He dresses hurriedly, the train is close. His shirt is mis-buttoned, there is no time for socks.

There's nothing Ed needs here. Pack it away, give it away, leave it behind. All he wants is his small vase of daisies.

The train rolls past, not too fast and not too slow. Ed takes hold of the handrail and swings up onto the steps at the end of a passenger carriage. He goes through the half-glass door and finding the entire carriage is empty sits by the window, facing towards the engine, holding the small vase of daisies carefully in his lap with both hands.

Although he cannot see forwards, when the train enters the tunnel he knows that even though it may be after miles and miles of darkness, there is the far tunnel mouth and that it shines with a soft light.

After all that rush for the train he's very tired. He closes his eyes and as he does, he remembers. He remembers everything, he remembers what was missing.

He remembers their name, and for the first time in an age he sees their face.

And although he is alone and riding through the darkest part of the tunnel he knows that up ahead they are waiting.

David Gullen is a two-times winner of the British Fantasy Society Short Story competition. His work has appeared in *The Best of British SF* 2020, and 2021, *F&SF, Tales from the Magician's Skull,* and more. Other work has been short-listed for the James White Award and placed in the Aeon Award. Born in Africa and baptised by King Neptune, David has lived in England most of his life. He currently lives behind several tree ferns in South London with his wife, fantasy writer Gaie Sebold, and the nicest cat you ever did see. Find out more at www.davidgullen.com.

Contact the BFS

The British Fantasy Society is run by many people, all unpaid, in their spare time. Here's a list of the email addresses for those currently involved. If you would like to contribute to the BFS in any way, then please feel free to email the appropriate person. If you would like to volunteer for a post, contact the chair.

COMMITTEE

President Elect — Juliet Mushens
president@britishfantasysociety.org
Chair — Shona Kinsella
chair@britishfantasysociety.org
Membership Secretary — Karen Fishwick
secretary@britishfantasysociety.org
Treasurer — John Dodd
treasurer@britishfantasysociety.org
BFS Horizons Editor — Pete Sutton
bfshorizons@britishfantasysociety.org
BFS Journal Editor — Sean Wilcock
bfsjournal@britishfantasysociety.org
Web Administrator — John Stabler (technical matters only, not content)
webmaster@britishfantasysociety.org
Events Coordinator — [vacant]
events@britishfantasysociety.org
British Fantasy Awards Administrator — Katherine Fowler
bfsawards@britishfantasysociety.org
Communications Officer — Jenn Arndt
communications@britishfantasysociety.org

Stockholder — [vacant]
stockholder@britishfantasysociety.org
Online Content Editor — Jessica Triana de Ford
online@britishfantasysociety.org
Reviews Editor — Sarah Deeming
bookreviews@britishfantasysociety.org
BFS Horizons Poetry Editor — Ian Hunter
poetry@britishfantasysociety.org
Short Story Competition — Steven Poore
shortstorycomp@britishfantasysociety.org

EVENT CONTACTS

London Events Organiser — Karen Fishwick
events@britishfantasysociety.org
Sheffield Events Organiser (in partnership with the BSFA) —
Steve Poore
steven.poore@hotmail.com
York Events Organiser (in partnership with the BSFA) —
Alex Bardy
mangozine@btinternet.com
Glasgow Events Organiser — Shona Kinsella
shona.kinsella@outlook.com

www.britishfantasysociety.org

Milton Keynes UK
Ingram Content Group UK Ltd.
UKHW020902211223
434772UK00013B/264